Haiti Shanghai

Lee Badman

Dedicated to Haiti, good Haitians everywhere, and all those from around the world who have cared enough to try to help after the big earthquake in 2010.

...Kidnapping is widespread, and victims regularly include U.S. citizens. Kidnappers may use sophisticated planning or take advantage of unplanned opportunities, and even convoys have been attacked. Kidnapping cases often involve ransom negotiations and U.S. citizen victims have been physically harmed during kidnappings. Victims families have paid thousands of dollars to rescue their family members.

Violent crime, such as armed robbery and carjacking, is common. Travelers are sometimes followed and violently attacked and robbed shortly after leaving the Port-au-Prince international airport. Robbers and carjackers also attack private vehicles stuck in heavy traffic congestion and often target lone drivers, particularly women. As a result, the U.S. Embassy requires its personnel to use official transportation to and from the airport.

Protests, demonstrations, tire burning, and roadblocks are frequent, unpredictable, and can turn violent. The U.S. government is extremely limited in its ability to provide emergency services to U.S. citizens in Haiti assistance on site is available only from local authorities (Haitian National Police and ambulance services). Local police generally lack the resources to respond effectively to serious criminal incidents.

   - *US Department of State travel warning excerpt*

Contents

Introduction

Haiti is a complicated place. If you stand in the right spot, it's as beautiful as anywhere in the Caribbean. Talk with the right Haitian people, and you'll be richer for the experience. But if you stand in the wrong spot, or talk to the wrong people, you may well get your ass kicked and see hell on earth. I would know, I've been there. I had some good moments there, I suppose. I enjoyed delicious food and marveled at the uniqueness of Haiti. But I also got pounded in the head with rocks, thrown in the back of a truck, and kidnapped. That dichotomy is what Haiti is all about, as I think about it. Ah well, at least I got to sing backup for rap star Ekselan Junior- even if I was a hostage at the time.

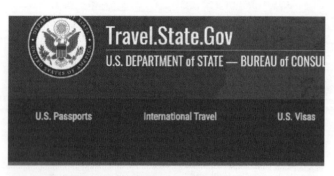

Travel.State.Gov
U.S. DEPARTMENT of STATE — BUREAU of CONSUL

U.S. Passports   International Travel   U.S. Visas

Travel.State.Gov > Travel Advisories > Haiti Travel Advisory

Haiti Travel Advisory

Travel Advisory	Haiti - Level 4: Do Not Travel

Do not travel to Haiti due to **kidnapping, crime, civil unrest,** and

Chapter 1: Fools Rush In

Looking back, it was a trip that probably should not have been taken. But as is the case with many ventures that go off the rails, it all started with the best of intentions. The country of Haiti got utterly devastated by the big earthquake in 2010 and people wanted to help. That's admirable, but it's also not that simple. Nothing in Haiti is simple. It's been a few years now since that crazy trip, and I promised a good man that I'd eventually tell the story. It's a doozy for something that was just supposed to be a work trip.

At the time, I was "an IT guy" for McDermott University in upstate New York. That's the simple version of what I did. Drilling in a bit, I was a senior network team member, with job title of Network Architect. I designed and oversaw a massive wireless network and assisted on everything else from security to troubleshooting some of the hardest network issues. Our CIO was a great guy, named Claude Sherman. Out of necessity Claude was connected to the academic and financial sides of campus as well, and he was approached by a "Help Haiti" committee made up of mostly faculty from different departments who had various ties to the Caribbean. There was one nice professor lady from Jamaica. And there was a fellow whose family fled Haiti when he was a child in the middle of the night ahead of the government hit squad that was coming for them over some political issue with his father. Then at least a couple of faculty members whose parents were from somewhere else in that region also wanted to get in on it. They had already collected money and sent some much-needed supplies down to Haiti, but they were looking to do something more *meaningful,* like seeing an IT guy get his ass beat in the mean streets of Port-au-Prince… All right, let me back it up a little and dispense with the sarcasm as there's plenty of time for that later.

I'm Howard Burlingame, by the way. My McDermott group had the goal of partnering up with a Haitian university and helping them to rebuild their programs after they lost faculty and facilities to the quake, and to install some basic networking to help them get restarted after the destruction of what little IT infrastructure they had. It really was a noble goal, and I was brought into it early on. Claude asked me if I wanted to be a part of the effort, as I had a good track record of getting a lot of work done quickly under unpredictable conditions in our satellite campuses in other parts of the US and in Europe. I honestly can't say I was immediately thrilled at the idea, and I told him that I'd give it some consideration. At the same time, I thought the world of Claude, and if he was going to Haiti, I knew in my mind that I'd be going as well.

But I needed to do some research.

Out of the entire group, I was the only one who had been in the military and who had been to places in the third world where Americans aren't always welcomed- or if they are, it's often because they make great hostages or send a powerful statement when their bodies are shown hanging from bridges. I dug around online for State Department warnings about Haiti and found plenty or reasons for concern. The US Embassy couldn't do much for Americans who found themselves in trouble there, and they minced no words in saying as much. The advice was simply "don't travel to Haiti or you risk likely kidnap or murder". It was never a safe place to begin with, and the quake only made it worse. There were plenty of articles to be found about people meeting an ugly end in Port-au-Prince shortly after they got off the plane.

Every part of me said "no"- to this idea except the part that didn't want Claude to be having an adventure without me along for it as well.

I made a feeble attempt to talk the group out of getting into initiatives that required our physical presence in Haiti. I forwarded the State Department warnings, but I was waived off by the faculty. They chalked those warnings up to the US somehow trying to *keep poor nations down,* or some such bullshit that I did not really comprehend. I didn't want to quibble with academics who had their own world views, being a lowly veteran who has actually tasted danger.

That sort of argument often goes nowhere with the ignorantly idealistic. The truth was that there would be no derailing an eventual trip down to Haiti. Too much conversational, feel-good momentum had already gathered.

My part in the equation would be to find unused network equipment with life left in it that we had on hand and could donate, and to also cajole any of our network device vendors to kick in gear for a noble cause. Then I'd get all that stuff and any tools and other materials like network wiring, cable ties, and screws we might need shipped down in advance of our eventual visit, and we would eventually work with the Haitian folks on the other end to set it all up. Meanwhile someone else from McDermott would be finding and working with a needed university in the country to get a relationship started. Wheels were turning on many fronts.

Meanwhile, I continued researching Haiti. I wanted to know more what I was getting into. What was really behind those state department warnings? Like I said, I had been in the military for a while, and had been to a number of third world places lacking in stability. But it's a whole different situation being someplace dangerous with your fellow soldiers and with the full backing of Uncle Sam; that's a pretty significant security blanket. This trip to Haiti would be nothing like that at all, by my calculation. After reading about specific cases of kidnap and murder, I determined that a lot of those could have been prevented with even a little bit of common sense and better planning. That provided a small bit of comfort. I convinced myself that if nothing went wrong, it *could* be a pleasurable and meaningful trip for our group. But I knew that if anything *did* go wrong, we'd be in deep shit pretty much instantly with no one to really turn to for help. I got the vibe from the rest of the team that we really weren't supposed to entertain that sort of thought on this venture to Haiti's biggest city, Port-au-Prince. This was supposed to be all sunshine. I just couldn't put their blinders on, but I did keep my mouth shut about my concerns for the most part after my initial offerings were shut down.

After having seen it, I describe Port-au-Prince's geography as somewhat akin to a giant bowl, except where it is bordered by the waters of the Gulf of Gonâve which opens up to the Caribbean Sea. Almost a million people live on the bottom and sides of the bowl. Beyond that bowl, the country of Haiti itself is shaped somewhat like an open crab claw, with a north and south section protruding east out into the sea around the Gulf of Gonâve. The Atlantic is on the north coast, with the Caribbean Sea to the south. Haiti is the small half of the island of Hispaniola, with the Dominican Republic making up the larger half. Haitians identify more with the French and speak either French or Creole, while Dominicans speak

Spanish. Both countries have histories far older than the United States' own. Hispaniola and the surrounding area are beautiful from the air, but the closer you get to the deck, the less pretty it all gets in spots.

Back to Port-au-Prince- and the "bowl". Everything and everyone in it were all hit hard by the earthquake. Like, harder than you can possibly contemplate without seeing it for yourself. Even then, your mind may not be able to process the extent of the devastation. If you are familiar with tornado damage, you might say that it looked like a tornado as wide as you could imagine hit *everything*. I'd eventually learn that other parts of Haiti also took their share of damage, but our interests on this university trip were in Port-au-Prince proper where the density of population and poorly built buildings particularly exasperated the scale of the damage. It felt very much analogous to a war zone when I saw it. Tragedy was in the air, and destruction often filled the eye.

The government in Haiti seems to get violently overthrown every so often, and hand-offs of power from one president to the next are frequently accompanied by bloodshed. On our trip, Michel Martelly was the president. He struck me as a decent guy. Haiti also happens to be the poorest country in the Western Hemisphere, existing under perpetual dark clouds of sickness, natural disaster, and ill-executed foreign intervention. Corruption is rampant, and the *Police Nationale d'Haïti*, or Haitian National Police, are pretty much it for law enforcement and anything close to national defense. This agency also sees its share of exploitation by nefarious members. I did a lot of reading about the country in the weeks leading up to the trip. But no matter how much you prepare to go to Haiti, you're never really ready for what you find when you get there.

Eventually we did get there. But first there were dozens of emails and calls between us and our new friends at *Université Affiliée d'Haïti* (UAH), the Affiliated University of Haiti, setting things up. The plan was that there would be the initial meet-and-greet, tours of a couple of small UAH campuses, work planning, and eventually getting our equipment out of customs and doing some network installations while the faculty folks worked on academic partnerships between McDermott and UAH. On paper, we'd be helping potentially hundreds of college students to minimally get back to where they were before the quake hit while possibly also doing some future scholarships for their students. That was the basic agenda.

Haiti plans don't always go smoothly though.

We made the entire trip by air in maybe six hours total. Out of Rochester to Charlotte, then on to Port-au-Prince's Toussaint Louverture International

9

Airport. I learned that commercial aircraft back then as a rule flew to Haiti with enough fuel to also continue on to their next destination given the damage to airport facilities from the quake. The engines on the aircraft were never turned off. Also, there was minimum contact made with the aircraft by people on the ground, out of security concerns. No jetways were used, and the flight crew did a lot of the tasks that normally a ground crew would- and with great haste to minimize their time in Haiti. Some haste was because they wanted the reduced airfield available for relief flights, but it also seemed to me like aircrews just wanted to get the hell out as fast as they could lest they get stuck there. As we approached Hispaniola in flight, it was easy to marvel at the beauty of both the Atlantic Ocean and the Caribbean Sea from cruising altitude. The blues and greens from the air were otherworldly. That beauty rapidly burned off, however, as we descended into Port-au-Prince, and I saw the bleak enormity and somber condition of the city. I had a vague sense of how rough it would be before we travelled but like anything in life, it's a different game when you finally get there and are in the situation.

Landing was interesting in a couple of ways. In Charlotte, most of the passengers that boarded were Haitian. As soon as the aircraft's wheels made contact with the runway, cheers erupted like a winning goal had been scored at a soccer game. It was absolutely raucous. And even before we slowed down to taxi speed, most of the Haitian passengers were out of their seats and clamoring over each other and the rest of us to get into the aisle. The flight attendants didn't even bother to ask everyone to sit back down, the situation was too far gone. I still don't understand what that mad hurry was for to simply stand in the aisle, but it seemed perfectly normal for those taking part in it. It felt odd to be climbed over, but those doing the climbing made it seem like it was normal to them. Both the front and back of the aircraft were used for rapid deplaning, and we had a long walk across the ramp to get to the airport- or rather what was left of the airport. Simply getting off the plane and setting foot on Haitian ground was a bit of a shock to the system. The heat, the bright sunlight on the strange-to-you landscape, and the noise and smells of being directly on the flight line kind of slapped you upside the head.

The airport terminal was the first building that I would see up close that was hit hard by the quake. A huge section of it looked structurally off-kilter, with windows broken, walls obviously damaged, and rooftop fixtures laying in pieces. The part of facility that did stay in service wasn't much better off. Ceiling tiles were hanging from their frameworks, there was no air conditioning for dealing with the tropical heat, big sections of interior space were roped off with various signs of damage beyond the barriers, and there were just far, far too many people in any given few square feet. It took a couple of hours to get our luggage, and to clear customs. All of that was hot, chaotic, and came with sensory overload. Finally, our group had corralled everything we had brought, and our UAH contact led us back outside into that bright tropical sun and eventually to a bus which was more like a large van.

Walking to the bus was also a bit frenetic. One person after another was trying to sell us trinkets as we passed by, others were trying to engage in conversation in French for reasons we'd never understand, and there were just people *everywhere*. There must have been half-mile queues of Haitian folks waiting to leave the country, with lines stretching way out of the airport. The small bus itself provided little relief from the chaos, as it was cramped for space and not in great mechanical shape. But at least we were on our way to the hotel.

The *Le Festival* resort and hotel would be our base of operations during our stay in Haiti. It was only four driving miles or so from the airport to the Petion-ville neighborhood where the hotel was located, but it took at least forty-five minutes to get there from the condition of the roads and the sheer madness of Port-au-Prince traffic. There was plenty to process along the way including endless tent and tarp villages for as far as the eye could see up the hillsides, dizzyingly colorful tap-tap trucks overcrowded with passengers, little roadside stands, and rubble everywhere there wasn't a crater. I tried to make sense of what was normal Haitian society among the added chaos of the quake aftermath, and found that I had a hard time finding the demarcation. In the distance, buckled buildings loomed, and up close to the streets people carried baskets of who knows what on their heads and pushed carts full of sugarcane. Occasionally you'd see an individual urinating where they stood- both men and women. There was also the occasional United Nations Range Rover or Land Cruiser, and Haitian National Police trucks and motorcycles with heavily armed officers looking bored with it all as columns of traffic passed them. It was a lot to take in.

Petion-ville is a fairly upscale neighborhood once you turn off of the public roads, and it exudes an affluence not present anywhere else in Port-au-Prince- at least not that I saw. Le Festival was supposedly one of the hotels where diplomats stayed when visiting the country, and it felt quite first-world. The next hotel over had a helicopter on the roof, and up in the hills above the resorts you could see very nice houses with large yards, tennis courts, and swimming pools. It was much the contrast to all that we had seen in the city coming from the airport. Any damage that may have hit Le Festival and nearby buildings was relatively minor or already repaired, as the complex was fully operational and really lovely by any country's standards. We all got settled into our rooms, and eventually had our first meal at the hotel restaurant.

I learned long ago in faraway lands that no one *anywhere* likes arrogant, pushy Americans in their establishments. From the time I stepped into the hotel restaurant, I made sure to show respect and courtesy to the hostess, Fabienne, and to the waiter Robenson. It got me a drink and a menu quicker than some of my colleagues who didn't quite catch on that these situations are different when you are away from American soil. Like almost everyone in Haiti, they called me "Mister Howard" rather than just Howard. Basic courtesy and a friendly rapport with them would eventually prove to be a profitable investment in goodwill that reached beyond the hotel.

I'd learn that Fabienne and Robensen were siblings, and that Fabienne ran a tight ship outside of the kitchen when it came to serving customers. She had a subtle, almost imperceptible way of prioritizing individual customers based on how they treated the staff. Once you caught on to it, it was somewhat amusing as the worst offenders may not even get a glass of water while the other patrons at the same table were well into their meals. When Fabienne realized that I was on to her, she blushed beautifully. I liked talking with her and Robenson both very much when things were slow and we all had time to chat. I can say that every meal served at Le Festival was both delicious and beautiful to take in with your eyes.

Our McDermott contingent got a few days into the relationship with UAH, and interactions were going along well enough, despite the fact that pretty much every assumption we had made before the trip was proven wrong. It took a solid couple of workdays just to get to where we understood the current state of the modest and damaged network environment at UAH, and how we might be able to put together something of value for them at a few of their small campuses distributed around the city. All efforts we had made to get this information before hand was either lost in translation or we just didn't talk to the right people as we found our research to be almost worthless. We finally got to a point where we could be productive.

Then things went to shit for yours truly.

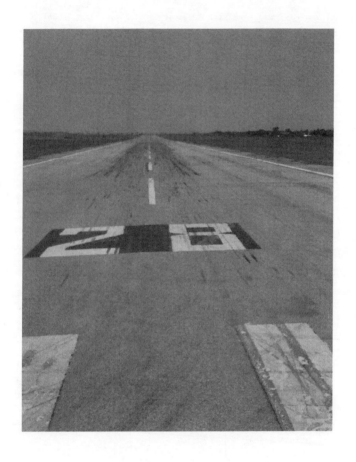

Chapter 2: Never Get Out of the Boat

While traveling around throughout my adult years, I've developed a few minor phobias that I don't mind admitting to. For instance, I always have a small flashlight in my carryon baggage when I travel in case the airport is suddenly plunged into darkness. Sure, it'll never happen, but somewhere I developed an odd little paranoia in that regard. Another one is having the group that I'm traveling with not be split up when overseas, under any circumstances. The group is strength, and it's protection- even when that group is comprised of mushy academic types. You take what you can get. On this trip, we all agreed that we were to never be less than a group when we travelled, by our trip charter. If we needed to split up, it would be into two smaller groups and each would be accompanied by a couple of staff from UAH. No one would be solo at any point, and there would be very little exploration of public markets and such unless done as a group with multiple escorts. That was the generally agreed upon plan.

But this was Haiti, where plans are fragile and subject to rapid and radical change. We found ourselves in a situation where after days of spinning our wheels, we were suddenly getting a lot done collectively. We were gaining momentum and feeling good about that, and so we all forgot about the agreement that we'd stay in a group. I went off to another UAH campus to do some work by myself, driven there by a nice fellow named Frantz. He was a UAH staff member. I was so focused on the tasks at hand that I didn't think anything about being separated from my peers. That is, until it was time to depart after accomplishing what I went to the other campus to do. At that point I realized that I was suddenly the lone American in the very sort of situation I had feared would develop. I tried to keep my anxiety at bay. Then I started thinking about a scene from the movie *Apocalypse Now.*

In that scene, Captain Willard and Chef are in the jungle gathering mangos, taking a quick field trip away from their river patrol boat. A tiger charges them, but Willard calmly dispatches it with his M-16. Chef is wound way too tight, and he is going nuts. He sprints back to the boat yelling all kinds of unintelligible gibberish (*fuckin' TIGERRRRRR aaaaagh*). The rest of the crew on the boat starts firing into the jungle thinking that they were under attack by the Vietcong, based on Chef's crazed, terrified antics. As Willard calmly takes in all the foolishness of the situation, Chef utters "Don't ever get out of the boat, man!" Then Willard puts a finer point on it as he narrates the end of the scene:

"Never get out of the boat. Absolutely goddamn right. Unless you were goin' all the way."

18

I realized right then that I had gotten out of the boat, so to speak. I really wanted to get back on it. I wasn't interested in finding out what *goin' all the way* might amount to. Captain Willard's voice kept playing in my head, telling me I shouldn't have gotten out of the boat as Frantz and I got in the truck to make our way back to the group. I couldn't find a way in my mind to make Captain Willard to shut up.

I'm guessing I was no more than a few miles from the others from McDermott at that point, but that equals at least a half an hour at best on Port-au-Prince's brutal streets. Frantz did a great job of picking his way through immense potholes and negotiating traffic snarls, and the little pickup truck we were in was much more comfortable than the bus that carted the whole group around. I kept telling myself that we were almost there and all would be well. We were making small talk as best we could and getting into the thick of an urban neighborhood when Frantz made a right-hand turn. He got maybe half a block, and then there was an obvious problem. Frantz very quietly said *"Mèd"* (fuck) as he rolled to a stop and we both took in the scene in front of us.

I couldn't tell what the road was blocked with. Burning tires? Burning body? It could have been either or both, but the burning was definite as was the unpleasant odor that came with the smoke. Yelling around us was getting louder, and Frantz put it in

19

reverse to get us out of there and said something like *"I'm sorry, Mister Howard, hold on"*. Then the rocks started flying. Suddenly it was combat, and we were unarmed. The truck was getting pelted with an onslaught of stones about the size of apples, or maybe grapefruits. The back window on my side was shattered pretty quick, and the whole truck was just taking a beating. I put my backpack up to the window to try to shield my head. Frantz' window was open, and a rock whizzed in just missing him, it bounced from the steering wheel and caught me upside the head on my left cheek and temple. Then the windshield was cracked in several spots, my window was shattered, and we stopped moving. I looked at Frantz, and he was slumped over the steering wheel. In the second or two that I let my ears do their job, I heard more angry yelling, the pounding of the rocks against the truck, and what could have been small caliber gunfire- like .22 or .32 or best. Without thinking I opened my door, pulled the very limp Frantz across the cab to the passenger side, and ran for the driver seat to try to get us out of there.

I didn't make it. Suddenly my head exploded with pain. As everything went dark for me, I heard Captain Willard telling me *"You're about to be goin' all the way, Howard..."*.

Fuck you, Captain Willard.

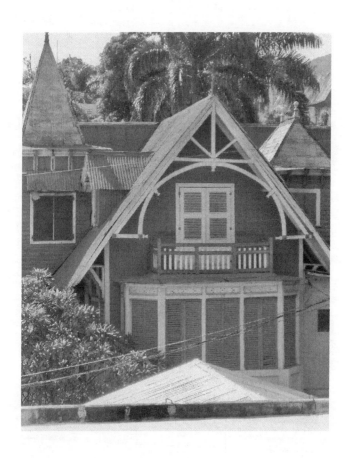

Chapter 3: Hostage (or Guest?)

As bad as what happened was, I suppose it's made even worse by knowing that it was coming. I think I felt on some level that this whole damn mess was in the cards for me long before we even left the states. Call it premonition or self-fulfilling prophecy, whatever. I just sensed *something* was going to happen. I didn't know how exactly, just that it was going to. And now here I was.

When I woke up after the attack, I was quite disoriented. Once my eyes dialed it all in, I was surprised at my surroundings. I'd have expected to find myself in a shack somewhere with an ugly guard glaring at me over a crappy old gun, like out of a movie. But I was in a decent bed, I had an IV in my arm and a bandage on my head, and the room was modest but clean. And there was no one else in it. I heard no sounds from anywhere else in the building.

I worked myself to sitting up, to see how my head felt. Thankfully, it was a dull throb at worst. Looking around the room, I saw a vial of pills with no label on them and a couple of bottled waters. I was in the same clothes I had been wearing when the rocks were flying, and there was a fair amount of blood on my shirt that looked like it had been dried for at least a solid day. Someone had cleaned up my head- I wasn't feeling any matted blood in my hair or near the gash I knew was there. That was certainly sporting of whoever had me here. Overall, I wasn't feeling so bad... fluids were going into me and a pound of gauze was on my head. I didn't see a place to pee, but I really had to go. I stopped the IV and took it out of my arm, then noticed the little camera up in the corner. I stared at that for a little bit, and then I spoke to it, *"Hello? Anyone there? I really need to use the bathroom".*

Nothing happened. No doors opened, and I assumed I was locked in. Yet I had to piss before I made a mess of the bed and myself. I moved the curtains and saw a balcony. That would have to do. I opened the sliding door and stepped out into the light- it felt like late afternoon maybe, with some rain probably coming. My bladder was about to explode, so I took care of that before I could process much else. After I did my business, I tried making sense of where I was. It looked like I was at least three floors up in one of those "gingerbread houses" that are a fixture in Haiti. These buildings were first built in the early 1900s for prominent Haitian families and businessmen, and are usually big, ornate in color and design, and typically clustered in neighborhoods in cities like Port-au-Prince and others around the country. My newly-pissed on house was certainly ornate from what I could tell from the balcony, in a pale yellow color with some funky blue and green accents in different

24

spots. But I clearly was no longer in Port-au-Prince, and I didn't see any other houses nearby.

Looking out farther, I could see the seaport at Port-au-Prince way off in the distance. Then the city worked its way up to the base of the mountain directly in front of me before giving way to forests and ravines. The view was impressive- I was above *everything*. On the periphery, I could see a slew of radio towers, which I had noticed from down below before the attack. It was on the McDermott agenda to come up to this area with our UAH colleagues to look at potential locations for wireless bridge links for a couple of their campuses. I supposed it was Mount Boutilliers, and I recall that if that was in fact the case it was some seventeen miles from Port-au-Prince, or less if we came up from Petion-ville directly from the hotel, from our planning.

My mind was all over the place, playing back the attack and trying to get grounded on where I was. I remembered Frantz sprawled out in bad shape. It had been a lot of years since I was anywhere near that sort of violence and seeing somebody potentially dead at arms-length. I was trying to reconcile the primitive brutality of being pelted with stones in the middle of loud riot chaos with where I was now, in this quaint, quiet little room with a nice view and a balcony that was just right for peeing. Whoever had me now provided basic medical care, and they had a camera that may or may not have been working. It was a lot to chew on. And on the topic of chewing, I was starving. I stepped back into the room, and a well-dressed Haitian man, maybe in his early 40s, awaited. He spoke perfect English, with a French accent that was more pleasant than distracting.

"How are you, my American friend?"

I asked if were in fact friends. I also thanked him for the medical care, and said I hoped that he wasn't the one who created the need for that care.

"On behalf of my countrymen, I apologize for your injuries, Howard Burlingame. You suffered a concussion, and you'll find that one of your molars was broken. I assure you that my organization had nothing to do with you being attacked."

Hmmm. Now I was curious. "What is your organization, sir? And do you have a name?"

"I am John. You and your Haitian friend had the bad fortune of driving into an area where a protest was happening. When the citizens are angry, no one is safe in a protest. Not children, not the elderly. The area is a war zone during a protest. Everyone is a target. It's basically madness. You have become yet another victim of the infamous Hatian protests."

I asked John if he knew what became of Frantz.

"He was not hurt as badly as you. Our men stepped in before the gangs killed him, and he is at his home. The truck is gone though."

I was happy to hear about Frantz. But I still had no clue who John was. I asked "are you with the police or an NGO? I'm not in a hospital, please forgive my confusion."

"I would certainly be confused also if I were in your place. No, we are not an NGO. We are... You can think of us as people recovery specialists? Yes, I like the way that sounds. The street gangs almost had you, and you would have certainly been a hostage at that point. With your injuries, it could have turned bad for you. We got to you first, and our men beat the person who smashed you in the head with the rock. Then we brought you here. I am trained in field medicine, but what's important is that you seem to be all right now, Howard? May I call you Howard? How do you feel?"

I felt generally OK, physically. But something else was wrong, that I couldn't put my finger on. I was thinking and speaking OK, but my mind was trying to reconcile why my internal self-check was failing. Meanwhile I thanked John. "I think I'm OK. I'm also in your debt for saving me, whoever you and your group are. Have you been in contact with the embassy or anyone about me? My group is staying at Le Festival in Petion-ville. Can you let them know I'm OK before we go there?"

I wasn't ready for what came next, not at all.

"Let me clarify. You are certainly not a hostage of a street gang. At the same time, we cannot simply take you back to your group. There is a rescue fee to be paid, and your medical bill. Also your lodging costs, and food and drink. You see, you are our guest, but we also need to be paid for our services. That is only fair, Mister Howard, yes?"

We looked at each other for several seconds. Then I looked around the room again. At that point I noticed a metal ring on a pretty serious bolt in the corner of the room. That could only be for tying someone up.

"So I am a hostage. I see. Will you be contacting my group at Le Festival so they can pay and I can get back with them?"

"If only it were that simple. You see, we have contacted an associate in Florida who has access to a number of resources in the US. We need to figure out exactly who Howard Burlingame is so we can either charge the appropriate rate before setting you free, or figure out what agency to hand you off to. You could be anyone, here for any number of reasons. So, we must dig for the truth. I know that this must sound frustrating, but I can assure you that no harm will come to you as long as you are a well-mannered guest. We will free you in good health once your account is settled. Do you understand?"

"I'm trying to understand. I'm assuming you've seen my driver's license and my university ID? My passport is back at the hotel if that helps."

"Certainly, you have documents. We all do. That is to be expected. But in this world, sometimes there is more than the eye can see. We will... investigate the situation. Meanwhile, be comfortable, Mister Howard. Rest in the bed, enjoy the fresh air on the balcony. Behave yourself. Make no mistake, I am a gentleman who is capable of being anything but a gentleman. My associates in the house are not to be crossed either."

I locked eyes with John, and then it dawned on me- what was not quite right inside me.

I understood everything he was saying, but I felt no worry or concern. I truly did not give a shit.

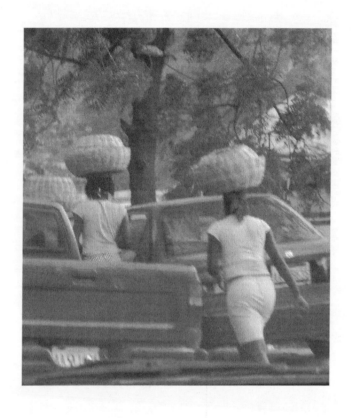

Chapter 4: Off to an Odd Start

I said to John, "so let me play this back to you… and tell me if I've missed anything. I was *almost* taken hostage by a low brow street gang and I may have ended up dead had that happened. But luckily for me, a much classier group of captives is holding me. We're not going to call me a hostage, but that's what I am. I'm a paying guest whether I want to be or not here in John's Hotel. And I better watch my step and not piss you off. Is that all accurate?"

"I don't blame you for being angry. But this is our current situation, yes."

As John moved around the room, I noticed the small bulge under his shirt on his right hip. That was probably no larger than a .380 semi-auto. That didn't really change anything for me- I wasn't about to do anything stupid, whether my head was injured or not. It was a strange situation to process, but I just couldn't muster anger or really even concern.

"Here's the thing, John- I think something happened when I got hit on the head because I can honestly say that I don't care right now. I'm not angry. I'm not frightened. I should give a shit or be scared for my safety given that gun you have, but I'm not. I am really hungry, though." It felt strange to say the words. It must have been stranger to hear them.

John stared at me, trying to digest what I said. I could tell that he was puzzled, and honestly so was I. When I say that I didn't care at that moment, I really meant it. It's like that part of my brain got shut off or something. John said *"let's get you some food, then we'll continue this talk. We have joumou, if you'd like- pumpkin soup. And bread. And more bottled water, we don't need our guest getting stomach problems so don't drink from the faucets. Please enjoy as much food and drink as you'd like. That all goes on your bill, of course."*

"Whatever. As a I said, I don't care. Serve me a wet newspaper and I'll eat it I'm so hungry. Charge me five hundred dollars and demand a generous gratuity. Whoopty-doo. *I do not care at the moment."*

John stared at me for a bit again and then he left the room, and perhaps twenty minutes later a nice tray of food arrived. It smelled so damn good. John carried it in, and an older, stern looking woman accompanied him. *"Eat"*, she more or less growled at me. That wasn't an issue, as I was famished. No one said anything as I made the soup and bread disappear. It was an awkward silence as they waited for me to fill my belly. Thankfully there was no real pain where my tooth got knocked out. Then the woman said something in French and John took my tray away. I waited for her to speak, and she was obviously waiting for me to do the same. So we stared at each other, then John was back with a second helping for me. As I ate slower this time, the woman said with a much thicker accent than John *"So you don't give a shit, Mister Howard. You are here with our food and medicine and a pillow, and you don't care. You have our hospitality in a nice room and YOU don't give a shit, Ungrateful Man."* She seemed pretty heated.

I told her she was spot-on as I finished off the second bowl of soup.

"Let's look at that wound on your head."

She came around behind me, tilted my head back, and suddenly pulled out a straight razor that she put snuggly against my neck.

"Now look me in the eye and tell me you don't give a shit, you rude American kochon (pig)!"

That wasn't a problem. Something had really happened when I got slammed in the head. My mind knew I should care that a thin layer of skin was all that separated my jugular vein from that surgical steel blade. But the concern just wasn't there. I couldn't find it. For all I know, it all leaked out of my skull and was laying in a puddle on that street in Port-au-Prince where I was attacked.

I looked straight at her and said "I'm sorry, lady. Like I told John over there, something happened when I got hit. I'd like to give you the satisfaction of scaring me to death, but I can't. There is nothing like that there in me right now. I don't like it any more than you do."

She let off the pressure of the blade a bit and seemed to be talking to herself as much as me. *"I have never heard of such a thing..."* She rubbed my head softly, like maybe your grandmother would.

"Yeah, well how many times have you gone to a foreign country to try to help people and gotten your skull smashed in by a bunch of angry assholes in the street? I'm guessing the results of that are going to be somewhat unpredictable." John looked at her, but I couldn't tell what he was thinking.

The blade disappeared to wherever it was hidden before, and now she was looking at the mess on my head for real. She winced a bit and disappeared out the door but then stepped right back in with a bottle of hydrogen peroxide. *"The bathroom is right out that door. No more pissing on the balcony like an animal, please. It eventually makes a smell."* She dabbed at the wound a bit and said it would be best to leave the gash on my head uncovered for a while and for me not to touch it. I thanked her for looking at it. Then John spoke.

"So you are... fearless, Mister Howard? After the hit to the head you know no fear?" He was still trying to assess whether I was bullshitting him, I think.

I told him that I didn't think that was the case. It was more like general deep apathy rather than fearlessness. It just didn't feel like I had any concern about anything, like I was dull in that part of the emotional spectrum. I told him that I was no Maslow but that I thought that concern needed to happen before fear could.

"So I tell you that your mother died. No sorrow? Or I bring you a beautiful woman to have... no desire?"

Since neither of those was actually happening, I could only speculate that they wouldn't register for me under the current circumstances. I truly did not seem to care about anything, more or less, as I observed my own behavior.

The lady eventually said that her name was Nina. Her and John did a lot of back and forth in French while glancing at me. At one point Nina actually chuckled a little bit before she left. She didn't say anything more to me, but she did touch my head again softly as if maybe she felt sorry for me as she made her way out. Then John said *"All right, man who doesn't give a shit. You should get cleaned up as best you can in the bathroom. There are washed clothes in there left behind by other Americans in the hotels and resorts, you should find something that you can wear. Do not try to leave this floor, please. We will talk more in a couple of hours. We have much to talk about."*

Whatever. I couldn't have cared had I wanted to.

Chapter 5: Probing for Limits

As I soaked in the tub, I pondered the situation. Being captive should be demoralizing, even when it's under the best of conditions. So far, my brief time as a hostage wasn't so bad. John was conversational even as he established that I was basically his prisoner, the soup was nice, and Nina didn't kill me. Those were all positives. But this apathy thing was strange, and I needed to figure out how far it went. I didn't know if maybe it was like short-term amnesia I had heard about, and perhaps something would trigger it away at some point. But then again, I'd never had what most doctors would probably call a traumatic brain injury. Haiti was proving to be great fun, just of the wrong kind.

The bathroom was fairly spartan but spotless clean, like the bedroom was. Tub and shower, commode, one wall shelf with towels and some clothes, and a very simple medicine cabinet with a mirror in front. There was a new toothbrush and travel-sized tube of paste for me, along with deodorant- all which of course would go on my bill. God only knows what the hell they would be charging for these items, or my meals. Ransom as a working concept was nothing I had the slightest clue about- who pays, how amounts are asked for and negotiated to some final bottom line, how payments were handed off or transferred- it all was beyond my experience and certainly didn't register as anything I really gave a flip about just then. It was simply too obtuse for my mushy head.

I remember that my eyes settled on that mirror on the medicine cabinet… and I thought I could probably break it pretty easy and use a piece to slit my wrist if I wanted to. I'm not sure why I thought about that, but my mind was going in some odd directions, and I was both participating and spectating as it did. As soon as the thought about the mirror came, another pushed it away saying, "I don't want to do that." Okay, that was interesting- I didn't care that Nina could have slit my throat, but I had a twinge of self-preservation when I thought about doing myself in. So there was some nuance to my apathy. I decided to do an experiment.

I got out of the tub and walked directly back to the balcony. No towel, no drying off. I didn't care that I was naked or wet or maybe on Hostage Candid Camera for all the people in the neighborhood to see. There was zero concern there, on any of that. I looked over the balcony and figured that I was maybe forty feet above the ground, given the high ceilings in the rooms and that I was on the third floor. I stepped up on the stone railing and stood there taking in the view from my new home probably on Mount Boutilliers. There was an airplane landing at the airport off in Port-au-Prince. I could see cars near the radio towers zipping along the road off on the periphery. The day was pretty lovely from where I stood there, bare-assed and drying in the breeze. I looked down again and leaned just a bit toward the outside and made myself think about just stepping off- but that same *I really don't want to die like that* feeling quickly came.

I stepped back down onto the balcony. So my brain wasn't completely broken, as I had no interest in suicide. I guess that was a start. Back in the room I went, and I sat down again. I tried to think through this strange mess in my head. I didn't care that I was naked. But I didn't want to die by my own hand. I had been hungry enough to ask for food, but really had no issue with maybe being bled out by Straight-Razor Nina. I was on the third floor of a big stone home, but didn't care what, or who, was in the rest of the house below. Supposedly John was in contact with someone in Florida who was helping to figure out what I was worth on the hostage market or if I was someone else pretending to be Howard Burlingame. A few miles away, my McDermott colleagues were probably losing their shit over my plight, making phone calls and maybe talking to an embassy that couldn't really help. Blah blah blah. Whatever.

Did I care that I didn't care? I thought about that a bit and the question seemed amusing for whatever reason to the point where I chuckled out loud. At that point I would have been a psychiatrist's wet dream. I guess I did care if I was bothering to mull it over. It sucks having your brain rewired without your consent. I was playing the part of patient and shrink in my own head high up on a Haiti mountain.

I knew that I *should* care about all of this because I was in a strange and dangerous situation, regardless of how well-spoken and well-mannered my captors were. I knew that I should *want* to think normally about clothing myself and maybe trying to learn more about this house and my overall situation. But if I tried to force it, my head hurt and could feel the immediate need to sleep. I realized I could control it all a bit if I just tried not to think about anything too much. I had no idea at the time how fast something like this would take to heal from- assuming that it would eventually heal.

I'd just have to wait it out. I decided to make myself at least survive. Nutrition, cleanliness, not provoking my captors, and those sorts of basics were my immediate to-do list. The rest I'd have to kind of go along with as it came. I found some of the hotel clothes that were a decent enough fit and got myself dressed. I've always been pretty adaptable, so I wasn't freaking out the way some people might be. I was there, like it or not. I looked over my head situation as best as I could in the bathroom mirror. It was ugly and swollen, but I also thought at the time that I'd had worse gashes before. I also fully realized that the more significant injury was under the surface and hoped that my brain hadn't been impacted too bad. I really had lucked out in getting decent basic medical care from these folks.

After my bathroom business was squared away and I ended my self-analysis session, I brought the small chair from the room out onto the balcony. It was really a gift being able to get sunlight and fresh air, and I had to remind myself that I was in a bad situation. With a stomach full of tasty pumpkin soup and clean clothes on my clean body, I fell asleep looking out over the city.

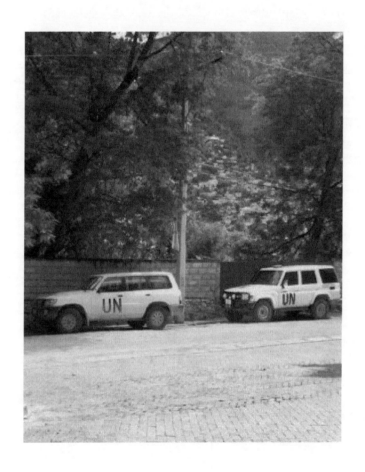

Chapter 6: Customs

I woke up, and I could smell cigarette smoke close by before I opened my eyes. I kept my eyes closed for a minute while remembering where I was and why. The chair wasn't particularly comfortable, but the air temperature and breeze were pleasant and made for a decent enough nap. I listened for any voices that might go with the smoke, but all was quiet. I wasn't ready for what I saw when I finally let my eyes open.

At the other end of the smallish balcony was a *Blue Hat,* a UN Peacekeeper with "POLICE" stenciled on his uniform, and a Jamaican flag emblem on his shoulder. He was alternating sips from a coffee cup and puffs on the smoke. He stared straight ahead and asked me if I wanted a cigarette. I recognized the voice.

"John? You're a peacekeeper?"

He waited a bit, then turned to me with a bit of a grin. *"As far as you know, Mister Howard. I need some way of getting around to certain places. Who is going to question a police lieutenant from Jamaica, mon?"*

"So… you're not a UN peacekeeper… and you're not Jamaican…"

"For someone who doesn't give a shit, you have many questions"

"Hey now- that was a statement, not a question. And I can't say that I'd care if you showed up looking like one of those ladies carrying sugarcane on their heads down in the streets. I'm just trying to digest what my eyes see. This circus is still all new to me."

"That is fair. But usually, the sugarcane is in carts. Those ladies carry other foods on their heads.   No matter though- If you're a good boy on our trip, maybe we'll get you some sugarcane to chew on. It's a novelty of sorts, and quite tasty. I'll even pay for that- it won't go on your bill!"

Hmmm. We were taking a trip. John didn't say where to yet. I did another quick round of personal bathroom business and then I got ready for my first trip out of that house. I did not care for one thing I was made to do- I had to put a black cloth bag over my head so I couldn't see as we went down a few flights of stairs. That was a ritual that would unfortunately become routine. John was very polite in guiding me around corners and telling me when to grab a railing and such with my sight blocked. He really was a nice kidnapper. He opened a vehicle door, helped me to not bump my head on the door frame, and told me to stay covered for just a little while more. From the feel of the seat and the height of the vehicle, I could tell we were in an SUV of some sort. John got in, started it up and over the sound of the smooth diesel engine I heard a garage door open.

"Stay covered just a few more minutes please. You're doing great, Mister Howard. I'm sorry about having to require that of you." My hands weren't bound, and the vehicle was very comfortable. John had a way of making me feel at ease in this very strange set of circumstances. He used his demeanor to his advantage, and I found myself thinking that it was hard to get angry at the guy. He seemed completely unconcerned with any move I might make towards him, but I got the sense that he could probably snap me in half like a breadstick if I pissed him off. I had no intention of testing that theory.

After maybe five minutes, John said I could take off the bag. We were well away from the house already.

"Welcome back to Haiti, Mister Howard. I'm John, I'll be your tour guide on this fine day. We'll be going down the big hill into the city of Port-au-Prince today, and your comfort is my priority. Of course, if you try to open the door and run, I will shoot you. But you really don't give a shit about that." He seemed to be enjoying himself.

I noticed the stubby machine pistol hanging from his shoulder. Maybe he wasn't a nice kidnapper after all. The look on my face must have given away my thoughts.

"Relax, Howard! I'm joking, although that probably didn't sound very funny from your perspective. Forgive me if my attempt at humor missed the mark. You are of no value to anyone if you are dead. But

there is also literally no place to run to here. The safest place you can be right now is with me, I think. Once we hear back from our friends in the States we can start calculating your fee, and you'll soon be back home mowing your lawn and going to McDonalds for fatty egg McSandwiches."

Whatever. I did mostly believe him that he was my best bet right now for staying safe. Unless he drove me to the front door of Le Festival and I jumped out and ran right in to Claude, I knew of no one to trust. The National Police may or not have been worth trying, and the thought of simply being on the streets alone as an American looking for aid with a dent in his skull felt pretty ugly. We were in a relatively new Range Rover with UN markings and very dark tinted windows. John's group seemingly had both deep pockets and gumption. He was absolutely just another United Nations' peacekeeper or official milling around the city to anyone noticing the vehicle. I asked if I could ask where we were heading.

"We are off to Customs, my friend. There is word afoot that you have some decent IT equipment there waiting. We're going to get it, and it may help with your future- but we'll talk about that later. I have your University identification card and as far as anyone knows we're just retrieving the equipment as part of your original plan."

This was weird. But that fog of apathy was still rolling through my mind and any of the hundred questions I should have had just stayed put. We were going to retrieve the equipment sent down from McDermott University before my coworkers and UAH did. I assumed that my colleagues from McDermott were fairly wrapped up in trying to find me and to work with anybody they could get a hold of from the State Department and such, and so they probably hadn't even thought about Customs and the equipment since I went missing. I was also assuming that with one person from our group already kidnapped, they probably weren't leaving the hotel much for anything. It did feel odd to be forced to commandeer my own pallets full of stuff, but at the edges of my thoughts I was curious where this would all lead. I was in a mystery of sorts.

We got into the thick of the city. Although I'd seen these streets before from the seat of the crowded UAH bus, it all seemed a little different riding through town with John in a cushy SUV. This was maybe five months after the quake had hit, and the devastation was palpable. But there were odd little things that jumped out at me that could have been fixed quick, especially after almost half a year. We were stuck in traffic for a few minutes, and making small talk, John asked me what I thought about it all.

I spoke without really thinking. "Its just sad. I understand that many, many people died. But look over there at the little roadside stand. The guy is sitting there waiting for customers, right next to the huge crater in the road. No cars can pull up there because of the giant hole, so they will go to another little stand. No one is parking half a block down to walk up to his little stand. I bet he goes days without business."

John looked at me, and maybe knew where I was headed by the look on his face. I kept going.

"So he sits there on his ass while no customers come and traffic gets tied up because of that big hole in the street. And right behind his stand is a giant pile of dirt and rubble. So why doesn't he fill in the hole while he sits there? It's not even ten feet away from the pile."

John thought before he spoke. *"That is not the Haitian way for many. We are used to people coming to our rescue, so sometimes we forget to help ourselves. Maybe it's all just too overwhelming for him. Many people are still shell-shocked from the earthquake."*

"Sounds like bullshit to me, John. He's not putting up a building. He's filling in a goddam hole. It would help everyone. He'd get customers and there would be one less traffic jam from vehicles having to go around the crater. Even if he got up once an hour to stretch his legs and kicked a little in dirt into the hole it would help, don't you think? If nothing else he'd get some exercise and eventually the hole would be filled in."

John looked at me with maybe derision for a moment. Then his look changed and he asked me if I wanted to fill in the hole. I said sure, I'd be happy to. I came to Haiti to help. Maybe if people saw what we were doing they might be inclined to do some of the same thing and pretty soon this sorry ass road would be easier to drive on. I thought for a second that maybe John would stop and we'd all be filling in a hole, but instead he pulled out his cell phone and called someone. Most of it was in French. It was low key but friendly. Traffic started moving a little again as he finished his call.

"We can't have you being seen out there filling in holes in the streets of the city, Howard. But by the end of the day, there will be several shovels brought here and someone will talk to the businesses. Maybe they will want to fill their own holes, then they can sell the shovels or pass them on to the next store in line. As you said, material is right there. Eventually the road will be properly fixed, but that could take years, and your suggestion is a helpful interim solution. That will be a credit on your bill." He didn't look at me when he spoke.

That was interesting on several levels. John knew people who could maybe get simple but important things done. He was connected and was obviously not just a kidnapper. And I'd earned *credit* against my ransom by simply bitching about people not helping themselves. You can't make this shit up.

We eventually got to the customs office building, which was not that far from the airport. It was a sterile, ugly industrial looking building that you kind of wished the earthquake would have hit harder instead of many of the beautiful buildings that were destroyed. It was on the corner of Rue something and Rue something else, and I'd never be able to remember those big French street names if my life depended on it. Into the fenced compound we went, and I was surprised how little activity there was given all of the relief initiatives going on from various groups. We stopped outside of an office and John beeped the horn quickly. A fellow came out, and John stepped away to talk with him briefly. I saw money leave John's hand, and I knew what was coming when he got back in.

"That was a bribe, and it goes on my bill no doubt. I'm paying to steal my own stuff."

John just smiled. *"At least you don't give a shit, my perceptive friend. That should be comforting on some level."*

We drove less than a minute down the length of the building to a huge garage door that opened for us, and John backed the Range Rover in. He told me it was OK to get out, and as soon as I did there was a machine gun pointed at me from less than three feet away. John and the fellow with the rifle obviously knew each other. A little light-hearted back and forth in French was exchanged, then John spoke to me.

"For the cameras, my associate here needs to keep the gun pointed at you. It is protocol. We'll open your

boxes, and you'll tell him what each item is. He doesn't speak English. But it's all for the cameras so his bosses know that he has inspected for contraband."

I'd be telling someone who didn't speak the same language and who was pointing an AK-47 at me what a bunch of IT equipment was, so it looked right on camera. OK, Haiti. I get it. There was no end to the foolishness at times. After I declared each of my items to an armed man who couldn't understand me, John would then put the boxes in the Range Rover, which was pretty cavernous with the back seat folded down.

Before we got started, I noticed pallets full of what appeared to be big Compaq-brand servers with a good coating of dust on them. I asked John what that was all about.

"That is Clinton Foundation garbage. They are supposed to be used in so many projects that will never happen, like repairing the seaports in Port-au-Prince and Cap-Haitien up in the north. We're supposed to take out huge loans for all these projects and then Haiti could never pay them back so we always are on the losing end. The last thing that will be needed is a bunch of obsolete servers and the other garbage that comes in with no coordination. People send this useless material to Haiti and then feel good that they did something to supposedly help, even though it is no help at all. I'd rather see shovels and

wheelbarrows and decent tents right now than old overpriced servers that will sit here for years with obsolete operating systems or eventually be sold for scrap metal. You are looking at pallets full of worthless politics! Fuck Bill Clinton and how he treats Haiti like his playground." John was pretty worked up. He was usually laid back, but those servers bothered him. I didn't understand the whole rant but I think I got the gist of it.

Then we started the charade of inspecting the McDermott equipment.

I couldn't get the plastic wrap off the pallet without a knife, so Machine Gun Joe gave me a boxcutter. That was gentlemanly. I asked John if I'd be charged for rental of the blade, and he smiled a bit and told me to be careful what I wished for. Then we got into the first box. I pulled out a wireless access point and held it up. I told the fellow who couldn't understand me what it was, and he dumbly nodded. Then I did the same with a small network switch. The charade was foot. After a couple more turns at this foolishness, I couldn't go on seriously. I held up another network switch.

"This is a George Foreman Grill."

"This is a papasan chair."

John was smirking, but he said nothing. Machine gun guy nodded dutifully after each item was presented.

"Sex toy"

"Jetski"

"Onion rings"

"Tickle-Me Elmo"

"Howitzer"

Eventually we got through it all. I returned the box cutter to the Customs guy after the last box. It was among the sillier exercises I've ever participated in, yet in a place where very little makes sense, it somehow made sense. The Range Rover was loaded to the gills, and we left.

John asked if I had seen the Presidential Palace before I was attacked, and I told him I had not. He said it was not to be missed, and to him was one of the most profound visuals that the earthquake viciously gifted to Haiti. We took a couple of turns down different streets, and what I suddenly saw before me was overwhelming.

Picture the White House in Washington DC collapsed upon itself, like someone removed the entire middle third of the building. Take the top third, and set it on the bottom third, kind of off-center. Even in its state of total destruction, the Presidential Palace in Haiti was still somehow beautiful. The white color was absolutely gleaming, the yards around it were vibrant green, and there were enough of the structure's lines left where your mind could fill in what it should have looked like before it was reduced to rubble. Without thinking, I heard myself say "it's heartbreaking".

I felt John glancing at me. He said nothing. Making our way a bit in silence, we passed the roadside stands again- and a couple of young men and one young lady were leisurely shoveling stones and gravel into the big hole. I saw John watching it all, but again we continued in silence.

Finally, he said *"Let's get a meal and you can explain to me how the sex toy connects to the howitzer and what we can do with that equipment back there."*

I reminded John that he promised me some sugarcane. He kinda looked at me odd for a few seconds then smiled somewhat. *"So I did. We'll get that on the way."* We made a couple of turns, and I noticed John scanning the busy street like he was looking for something. Then we made our way to one of the many little stands, and he pulled up as close as he could get us in the confusion of the busy street. He rolled his window down and yelled out at a boy named Ronald who came trotting up to the vehicle. John handed him some money, and there was a bit back and forth in French. Then Ronald hustled off to the stand, and he talked to a woman who then dug in promptly getting the cane pieces ready to nibble on. In a just a couple of minutes, the boy came running back over and handed John the goods. It was peeled and made ready for me, and John said *"enjoy your treat"* as he handed it t over. John and Ronald had another quick exchange, and Ronald again jogged off with a smile.

We both munched on sugarcane on the ride back up the mountain. Just hanging out with my captor, chewing on some native sweets.

Chapter 7: The Grilling

We went back to the house, and back to the balcony. Nina brought out some chicken and rice on trays, but it was *Haitian* chicken. Very chewy, without a lot of tender meat. I didn't care, it was nourishment. It was far better than what the countless poor bastards were probably eating in the tent cities that pervaded the area since so many apartment buildings were destroyed in the quake disaster. All through the hills, I had no doubt that tents were full of Haitians who didn't know what their own next meal might be. They'd probably love some chewy chicken.

John and Nina had lots of questions after our run to Customs. I got into the specifics of what the equipment now down in the garage could do. Provided there was an Internet connection available, you could make a fairly large single computer network, or many small ones. You might make it all simple enough in its configuration so it required very little support, or you could go crazy with features and security aspects that would require the skills of a network professional to keep it all going. Nina and John both listened intently, neither saying much at all. At one point, I asked for a pen and paper to sketch out a simple network drawing and John said, *"You IT guys live your lives in diagrams."* He seemed to be at least aware of everyone and everything.

After I had told them pretty much anything I could think of at a high at a high level about how the networking gear might get used, we had coffee in silence. Then there was a little bit of back and forth between them, and I kept hearing what sounded like "Internet café" in the exchange. At times it got a little heated, then silence while they both thought about the last point made. Then John's phone rang. He stepped back in the house.

Nina asked me how my head was, and I told her it hurt less than it did before but that I was getting headaches if I thought very hard about stuff. She asked if I still didn't give a shit about anything. I tried to clarify that I didn't have a lot of control over that, and I meant no offense to her and John about anything. She surprised me when she said *"I wish I didn't give a shit about so many things, Mister Howard. I could go to the ocean and swim and drink wine. It must be nice to not care about anything."* She was looking down the mountain to the sea, when John came back out with bottles of water for all of us and a busy-looking piece of paper in his hand. More French between Nina and John. John was reading the paper, and occasionally he looked at me quickly. Nina was waiting for John to digest what he was reading, and I got the definite vibe that it was about me. My background check or whatever the hell they were digging for must have come in from the States.

Suddenly it was on, like Donkey Kong. The two friendliest kidnappers in the world suddenly switched gears and I was hoping I didn't get waterboarded before we were done.

John took a deep breath, then spoke. *"So Howard Paul Burlingame... You were in the military for many years. You served in government. You own many guns."* I didn't hear any questions there, so I said nothing. I didn't realize that I was expected to speak, until Nina said *"we have all the time in the world, you realize. And time is money."* She sounded mildly irritated, and I told them I didn't pick up on what they wanted.

"You are a marksman. You were in the Philippines when the Marcos government was overthrown." John said this with as serious a tone as I had yet heard out of him, while Nina waited intently for me to answer. After I realized the implication he was suggesting, I actually laughed out loud before I could reply. That didn't score me any points by the looks on their faces, but I couldn't help it.

I told them how I was nineteen years old when I was stationed in the Philippines for the Air Force. Just a year prior I was in high school and living with my parents. I was an avionics technician and I worked on old F-4 fighters at my first duty station after training. *Everyone* who went through Air Force basic training and who was lucky enough to get a halfway decent M-16 at the range got the "marksman" ribbon, and once you had it, it stayed in your records even if you never qualified again. I assured John that as an Air

Force two-striper learning to fix aircraft systems I had nothing to do with Ferdinand Marcos being run out of the country, though I watched the events on TV. I had access to wrenches and radar components and oscilloscopes, not to weapons.

"And you were a government official?"

Wow. I had to fight back the urge to chuckle again. I explained that I was a Trustee in our little village in upstate New York, and I oversaw a three-person Department of Public Works. Three guys worked their asses off keeping up the streets and public water system while I tried to make sure they had budget for what they needed and that taxes were fair for the residents of the village. I did that for eight years, and when I pissed off the fire department over some minor funding disagreement I was voted out in an election where not even thirty people showed up. I told John I also coached Little League and worked with other community members at the annual Field Days doing chicken barbecues because that is what you do in small towns in the US. Nina and John exchanged glances. Then it was Nina's turn.

"You are a radio operator? Did you bring a radio with you on this trip, Mister Howard? Who do you talk to?"

I was starting to see where anything in one's "file" could be twisted into ill-intent if you were determined to see it. I was getting uncomfortable. I lived a pretty benign life, but to these people I was something exotic and potentially dangerous, it seemed. Yes, I have a ham radio license. I tried to explain the hobby side of it, and that on occasion I blabbered away with local folks on the drive in to work from my vehicle talking about a wide range of inane topics. On occasion I'd do the long-range stuff because it's fun to test antennas that you build, and for the last few years I was more just into listening to the police scanner and shortwave radio stations. All hobby-related, and no I did not bring a radio to Haiti because I did not know the laws of their country when it came to amateur radio. I told them I tried to see if the CONATEL website had any information on amateur radio and foreign visitors, given that the agency was akin to the FCC in the states. I found none, so opted not to bring a radio.

"Why do you own weapons? What do you do with them?"

I was getting irritated. I asked them if they were familiar with the Second Amendment, and American gun laws. They said they were somewhat aware of American freedoms, but still wanted to know why I had guns. I had learned how to deer hunt with my dad as a child. I also believe in protecting my family and property. I told them how I picked some guns up along the way at garage sales and such as I lived in other states during my Air Force time, and in New York the pistols needed to be registered. I told them that if I lived in a state other than New York, they'd never know that I owned guns because of different

63

gun laws about registrations. I had gotten away from hunting, but I still plink on occasion- target shoot- but even that was something I was doing less of from competing interests and the rising cost of ammunition.

"Do your university colleagues own weapons? Were any of them in the military?"

I was trying keep my cool, but my head was hurting and I felt a real irritation growing. How the hell would I know what they own? I barely knew most of them, and even that was because we were on this trip together. I told John I had no knowledge of what the others in the group owned or what their hobbies and backgrounds were and that he should get his person in the states to check on each one if he actually gave two shits. I was having a hard time not being a smartass with the line of questioning coming at me. I told him they were basically strangers to me, except for Claude. And even him I knew mostly through work. More glances between Nina and John. I got interrogated on all kinds of other things- places I'd travelled overseas, the one time I was arrested at fourteen for throwing a rock at a parked train (I thought that juvenile record was supposed to be sealed), and even my medical history. Whoever dug into my background had access to a crazy mix of information. The questions came fast, and sometimes they repeated- I guess to make sure I was being consistent. Eventually it seemed like their demeanors were returning to cordiality, like I had somehow exonerated myself for sins I had not come to Haiti to commit.

The conversation started to make my head hurt after a couple of hours. I said as much and mentioned half-jokingly that I could really use a beer. Nina said it was a bad idea in general with my injury, but then she seemed to reconsider and said that I could maybe have just one. She left the room. John said nothing more while she was gone, but he was deep in thought. Nina came back with two bottles of Prestige, which was a surprisingly good lager brewed right in Haiti. She opened one for each of us, and casually clanked her bottle against mine before we both sipped. She was doing a quick little toast with the prisoner she was interrogating. These people were profoundly strange at times.

John asked me to join him on the balcony while he had a smoke, and he talked about the lights that were starting to come on in little pockets in the city below and on the hillsides in the tent cities. There were some cooking fires, but also some portable solar-powered streetlights among the tents.

"There have been many crimes against women and children in those tent slums. When the sun goes down, the devil himself walks those hills. Haiti is home to great men and women, Mister Howard, but we have our shame as well. Obviously, there is no electrical power out there. You don't want your wife or daughters to be out trying to find cooking wood...

Those solar lights have helped, but we need to get people back to real homes."

I don't think he was talking to me as much as he was thinking out loud. I wanted to say that we have some real scumbags in the US as well, but I stayed quiet and just listened to this curious man.

"Before the tents there were bidonvilles, and the quake swept many of those cinder block shanty houses down the hills. People must go somewhere, must sleep and be somewhere so up went the tents. I didn't know there could be so many tents in the entire world. We need more of those lights..."

I noticed a rather large boat way out to sea on the horizon, and fast lights heading out to it. I asked John how the seaport was doing after the earthquake. He said it was hit hard with shipping greatly reduced, and that those boats were probably smugglers. I didn't ask what was being smuggled, and John didn't say any more. The beer was making me tired, and I think he saw that. I asked John if we were done... if they learned whatever they needed to set my price so I could eventually go home. He smiled and asked *"you don't like my company, Howard? Nina will be offended you want to leave so soon after your beer."*

He was a likable guy. I told him as much. "You two are both actually fascinating people. I like talking with you, even if it seems odd to say. I have no idea if you believe me, and like I said before, I don't really care. I have nothing to hide, and you are going to draw whatever strange conclusions you want about me. I can't control that. If I do get home eventually, any mildly-pleasant memory I have of this shit-hole country will be because of you. I know that sounds weird, but fuck it, I'm tired. And I'm swearing terribly in front of a lady. It's a bad habit I picked up in the military and I never had the good sense to leave it behind. Forgive me, Nina."

It would take more than my potty mouth to offend Nina. She smiled and said *"As you say, fuck it. You go get some sleep, Mister Howard."* They were avoiding my question. I still didn't know if my fee was decided on or if they had other weird stones to turn over before getting to that point. Whatever... I hit the bed and I was out.

Chapter 8: Tested

I slept solid that night but I was woken up around three in the morning by a Haitian National Policeman. My first thought was that the house had been raided and maybe I was being rescued, but it was far too quiet for that. As I focused on the policeman, I noticed there was a young lady in the room as well, setting up a small table. I said something like "what's going on?" and John's voice came out of the policeman's unfamiliar face.

"Good morning, sleepy head. Your services are needed today, but first we must get you properly prepared for the outing. This is Miss Esther, and she will help you become a new man. Please don't give her any trouble, she will be shaving your head and giving you a beard almost as wonderful as my own." He was stroking his newly applied facial hair.

So… John had a professional make-up person. And for wherever I was going, I too would be getting made over. I wasn't keen on getting my head shaved, but Esther made quick work of it and was extremely gentle around my wound. In around forty-five minutes, I was transformed into the bald, bearded man Peter-Paul Jensen, a Dutch IT contractor working with Global Comms- a fictitious NGO. I was a close-enough fit for the face on the ID that I'd be wearing after Esther worked her magic. I suggested that it didn't seem like I'd be released anytime soon if my appearance was being altered, and John told me not to jump to conclusions.

John was at least two inches taller than normal from lifted boots, and his HNP uniform was absolutely the real deal. So was the M1911 pistol on his belt, with three extra clips that were also very real. It was probably then that I started to appreciate this chameleon of a man, even if he was behind my lack of freedom at the time.

I was given a Global Comms dress shirt to wear, and then had to do the bag over the head thing as we went downstairs. Eventually we were on the road, and off came the bag. This time we were in a Toyota Hilux pickup, with full HNP markings. John explained that the rank he was wearing was *Inspecteur Principal,* and that we were on our way to the airport. Part of the airport network was down and there would be hell to pay there if the morning flights were disrupted. The throngs of Haitians who seemed to be a permanent fixture at the airport would not stand for a stoppage. John would be my police escort through the crowd, and he was hoping I might find the problem and solve it before the day's first departures.

Gee, no pressure there.

I attempted to explain that it can be hard to troubleshoot a network that you know nothing whatsoever about, without diagrams or analysis tools and a laptop. All networks are not the same, not by a long shot. John was listening, and kind of giving me the side-eye without saying anything as he drove. He seemed to be analyzing what I was saying. It was unsettling. I had no idea where this would go. I also couldn't make sense of how John of all people would be called for a network problem at the airport. Surely there must be IT staff somewhere for this sort of support need. The situation was weird, but I had little choice but to go with it. But it didn't feel right or realistic and it worried me greatly. I could not imagine what was going on then.

Going into the airport, even the service entrances seemed to be clogged with people. John picked his way to a somewhat-restricted parking area, and we walked into the crowded terminal. He asked people to give way, and if they didn't, my *Inspecteur Principal* escort made them wish that they had. John had no hesitance about getting brutally physical, and soon we were free from the crowd of people hoping to be lucky enough to get out on a flight to Florida where the biggest part of the Haitian diaspora was located. I was surprised how fast the mass of bodies was growing even at that ridiculously early hour. We walked over to the ticket counters. John said that only two of the terminals normally worked at all since the quake and that both were out of service that morning with whatever was now ailing the network. He said if they couldn't get people on flights in a little while, there would likely be all out rioting. Haitian people didn't seem to have any issues getting themselves worked up into a froth about any number of things, from what I saw. Physical violence was evidently just part of life there.

I approached the first workstation and found that I needed a local login name and password- which of course, John somehow had. I could not help but to frequently wonder who the hell this guy could be. After the first computer lit up, I found that it had no IP address. The second was in the same condition. I asked John if he knew where the server room or nearest data closet in the airport was. He led me down the corridor a bit and turned the handle of a door. It was locked. He asked me to position myself so no one could see him, and he made short work of picking the lock. He was a master of disguise, a tough guy, a very well-spoken gentleman, and now a lock-picker. John surprised me at every turn- kind of a Haitian James Bond meets MacGyver.

In the closet, I found the same sort of data rack setup you'd typically see at any business in any country that had a network. The station cables from the PCs came into a patch panel, and then connected to one of a few different Ethernet switches all mounted in a vertical row in the rack. The switches seemed all powered up with blinking lights. But then I noticed a problem with the main switch at the bottom that connected the rest of the switches to servers and routers in a different rack. That one was dead, with no lights. I mentioned it to John and asked if he knew if anyone would have a spare switch on hand in the airport. He just shrugged. I told him that even if we could find one, I'd have no way to configure it, or knowledge of how it should be set up. Out of desperation, I checked the power cord and found that it was backed out just enough to not make contact. I plugged it back in snug, and the switch came to life. John smiled and raised his eyebrows, but said nothing.

We went back out to the counters and found two very happy airport staff ladies working on the computers. They said something to John in French, and one of them squeezed my arm in thanks. I was glad that the situation turned out favorably, but that odd "what the hell is happening here?" feeling was hard to supress. We went to make our way out, and I froze. I couldn't believe my eyes. There was Claude and the rest of the McDermott group with their carry-on bags, getting ready to leave the country. They all looked tired and dejected. I stared at them, and John coughed softly to remind me that he was there. Claude looked directly at me in passing, but all he saw was bald-headed Peter Jensen of Global Comms standing there with a beard almost as magnificent as John's. I was a complete stranger. Then he sat down facing the other direction while waiting for his flight. I started to feel kind of shitty, both mentally and physically.

We headed down the terminal toward an exit, and the crowd was becoming thick, loud, and angry about something. I could see a fight in progress and growing into a proper melee, and the yelling was intense. Fists were flying, and I'm pretty sure I saw a glass bottle being swung at someone's head. I was getting a throbbing skull pain, and John hustled us out a maintenance hallway to a door that went outside. Day was breaking, and it was already getting hot. I suddenly felt like bloody hell and one step away from a meltdown. I stumbled a bit, and John helped me along back to the truck and got me a bottle of water from some compartment. We drove for a bit in silence, and as we did I felt a rage building along with the headache. John offered me a travel-pack of aspirin, and I knocked it out of his hand to the floor of the truck. He pulled into a half-destroyed gas station and cut the engine.

"You are very angry, yes?"

I lost it. There was no holding it in at that point. "Fuck you, John. Fuck Haiti…fuck Nina and Esther and the machine gun guy at customs. Fuck your shithole airport. Fuck this whole fucking fucked up place, you rotten fake fuck."

"That is a lot of fuck. I'm impressed, and I mean that", he said. John lit up a cigarette, and he offered me one. I don't smoke, but I took that one. It actually helped the head pain a little bit, at least temporarily. "Tell me what that was all about, John. Tell me why someone unplugged that network switch. Tell me why you wanted me to see my group leaving without me. Why fuck with me? I can't think straight as it is, now you're playing games? I came to here to help *your* people, and instead I helped you steal my own equipment out from under UAH. You shaved my

goddam head. Who the fuck *are* you people? You can go anywhere, and you can do anything. You can be any-fucking-body. Are you like with the fucking Haitian version of the CIA or the goddam *Illuminati* or something? Better yet, don't tell me. Fuck you. Did I mention that? In case I wasn't clear- go fuck yourself, John- or whoever the hell you really are."

He puffed. I puffed. I stared at him. He looked straight ahead. Then he finally spoke.

"You are not wrong, my American friend. The airport scenario was indeed contrived. We needed to make sure you are as you represent yourself. Many people we have... rescued... for a fee come to Haiti with elaborate cover stories and nefarious agendas. But you made short work of the scenario. You validated your credentials. I regret that you had to see your friends leaving, as that was not planned."

"Whatever. Take me back to my goddam cell and tie me to that big metal ring. I'm done with putting a bag over my own head and I'm done with your field trips out into this cesspool you call a city. I'm not an assassin or a spy or a smuggler or whatever the hell else you might think I could be with your asinine analysis of my background. You seem so smart, but you don't actually know shit about shit... Fuck you, brother. Put me on a fucking polygraph if you don't believe me. A guy like you probably has one under his goddam bed." I was ready to punch him in the throat and take my chances. I was livid.

Silence.

"You have looked under my bed, haven't you? I knew you could not be trusted." He smiled at his own joke, then took a deep breath. *"I will tell you a couple of things, Mister Howard Burlingame, and no more. UAH is a corrupt institution that has hands in many criminal ventures. Look into your contact when you get home. He is deported and banned from your own country- permanently. It is because you were doing business with him and his colleagues that you were on our radar to begin with, and why you are now with us. We assumed the worst about you and your party because of your relationship with UAH."*

"UAH certainly does not need your charity, but other groups here very much do and so you will help them. You will help Haiti as you came here to do. The Embassy knows you are safe in our hands, and your loved ones have been contacted. As for who I am... my organization is... we provide stability for the country we love while ineffective presidents come and go, and foreign companies exploit our leaders' almost constant ignorance. We have been all that stands between total collapse or takeover by the likes of China or Russia or even shitty weak countries like Cuba for centuries through continual struggle and disaster. In Haiti, we are the good guys. And ladies. Of that you have my word. Yet we don't exist. Do you understand?"

I did not. Yet I did. This was some secret society, or shadow government, or something. They did their own ransoming for money, yet they also seemingly had an altruistic mission. Maybe? They absolutely had an impressive operation from what I saw. If they had more men like John in their ranks, they must be a formidable group. Maybe they were propped up by the CIA or some such crazy shit. But then again, if it was the CIA behind them, it would probably have been more of an unsustainable clusterfuck. This group was polished and operated in Haiti by rules that only Haitians could understand. There would be no more answers to anything I might ask, so we rode back to the house mostly in silence. The only other thing John said was, *"let us go get some breakfast and we'll discuss how this adventure eventually ends for you."*

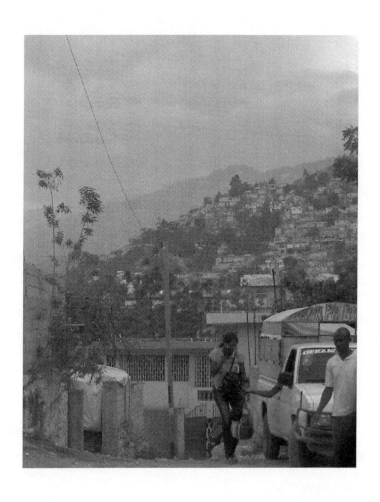

Chapter 9: Plans and Projects

I did end up doing the bag over the head again, like it or not. I would do so for pretty much every trip to or from the house. John looked me in the eye, and sincerely apologized but also said there was really no choice in the matter. He likened it to military protocol, appealing to my sensibilities as a veteran. When we got back to the house, I found myself in a different room with a large table, and Esther and Nina were both there with a table full of food for us. I was hungry, but Esther helped remove my fake beard before I ate. She was a master at that stuff. John kept his own on through the meal.

We enjoyed really nice plantains and scrambled eggs, with coffee and orange juice. There was very little conversation during the meal, except for some quick exchanges in French. I did ask "how do you all know that maybe I don't understand French? Perhaps I've understood everything you are saying." Nina didn't skip a beat. *"Every now and then I call your mother a whore or say that I'm about to kill you and feed your body to the dogs in French. You haven't shown any reaction at all. You do NOT understand French, Mister Howard, I assure you."* She smirked a bit. Fair enough. As we finished the meal, John asked if I could spend some time talking about radio topics with Esther.

To my surprise, Esther was an electrical engineer by training and education, as well as being skilled at make-up and disguises. She said that she had done some theater stuff before deciding to be a technical geek- her words. She wanted to talk at length about police scanners, and how to program them. I told her which brand and model scanners I had at home, and what software I use to program them. She took meticulous notes. She hinted that they had several models they were having trouble with, and it seemed very important to her to be able to use them. We talked about how complex these gadgets had become over time, interface cables, comm port settings on the programming PC, and which software worked best for me for each model. I also gave her a bunch of websites and forums that stayed up to date to turn to for help. She seemed very pleased as we talked, and I got the impression I filled in some of the missing pieces in her knowledge and made her less frustrated by knowing that someone else seemed to think they could be challenging to use. John halfway listened along, while also pecking out messages on his phone. After maybe an hour and a half, Esther dismissed herself and Nina brought in more coffee. I needed a bathroom by then, and Nina walked me down this hallway I'd never been in and waited outside the door to bring me right back in to the dining room.

John had his own notebook and pen ready when I got back to the room. It was obvious that he had something big on his mind. I sat and sipped my coffee while he drew a simple timeline. Then he spoke.

"We are here, today. At the end of this line, we will get you on your way home. But between now and then, we have a few projects to complete, if you will be so kind as to accommodate us. Understand that there will be no fee for your release, and you will also be somewhat compensated for your troubles and for your assistance." He paused for my reaction, but I was dumbfounded. I said nothing.

"Unfortunately, I can't query if this is acceptable- as there really is no option for you to decline or to negotiate. As you mentioned before, you still are captive. I realize how terrible this sounds. I assure you that you will be as safe in your work as possible, you will have assistance, and you will have our gratitude. Now for a civics lesson, Mister Howard...less than twenty percent of Haitians have access to the Internet right now- did you know that? You will help us get the Internet to some locations where it is most needed. And at the end, just a few days from now hopefully, you will be rewarded for your efforts. Then soon you'll be on your way home to watch Seinfeld reruns and drink Budweiser."

This was interesting. I told John I didn't drink Bud, and I really didn't care about Seinfeld reruns. But I was glad that my situation had changed from being a legitimate hostage to that of forced laborer status. I wanted to get the hell out of Haiti, but I was very

81

curious about the work I was now to do. My sense of adventure had been tickled a bit, and I also realized that I was in the presence of intriguing, mysterious, downright fascinating people in this strange country. Maybe I wasn't in so much of a hurry to get away from them, whether I wanted to admit that or not.

John said that we'd be setting up two Internet cafes- one with a handful of wired computers that people could use, the other with just Wi-Fi. In both cases a decent Internet connection (by Haitian standards) would be waiting for us. Esther retrieved a fairly comprehensive networking toolkit to show off and told me about various other supplies she had assembled for the work we'd be doing. I was impressed. We'd also be trying to fix an important small network that was down- that made three jobs. The final project would be talked about after the others were done as it was somewhat unique. There was no mention of locations, and I didn't ask. John did his best to describe the specifics of each situation and asked me to help Esther document them the best I could for future reference. We'd stage the equipment out of the UAH components one project at a time, and anything left over would be used as spares or for later things that I would not be part of. At each project site, there would be someone trusted on hand to both help and to then take care of what we'd be leaving behind. Esther would be along to see each project and to possibly lay hands on, and I got the impression that she was probably something akin to this group's Chief Technology Officer. That all sounded fine.

Then John said, *"Our first location will be very dangerous. You will be Peter Jensen again, and we will have several armed men around the building so please don't be alarmed about that."* I pointed out that he had just said I'd be safe in my work. He reminded me that he actually stated that I'd be as safe as possible *given the situation.* John looked me in the eye with a somber expression on his face. He added *"you will also be given a sidearm, Howard."*

Holy shit.

I was taken to my room, and I was blown away that my things from *Le Festival* were placed neatly on the bed. What the hell? There was a hand-written a note on top of the pile. It simply said *"Salut Mesye Howard, Fabienne"* with a smiley face underneath. Everything was there- my wallet, passport, clothing, toiletries, and even my cell phones. I had one for work and then my personal phone, but both had their SIMs removed. The place and its people were baffling. But I wished I could have thanked Fabienne.

I went out on the balcony to think. As I looked down over Port-au-Prince, I had to wonder where down there I might find myself next. Perhaps we'd be traveling out into other parts of the country. I had mixed feelings about all of this- I did not like having no choice about what I was about to be involved in, but I also thought it would be interesting to finally be able to do something of value in that goddam place. It was already absolutely the strangest trip I could ever imagine taking, and it was getting stranger. I couldn't help but think about other "guests" who may have been on this balcony or tied up to that metal ring in the bedroom, and I thought about how John threw people around at the airport without hesitation. I'd hate to be in this house as one of those people who went to Haiti for nefarious purposes but ended up there, right where I was, under less cordial circumstances. I'm guessing those folks didn't get pumpkin soup, beer, and John's good manners. Nor did their captors likely promise to furnish them with a weapon on a tough job site.

Ah Haiti.

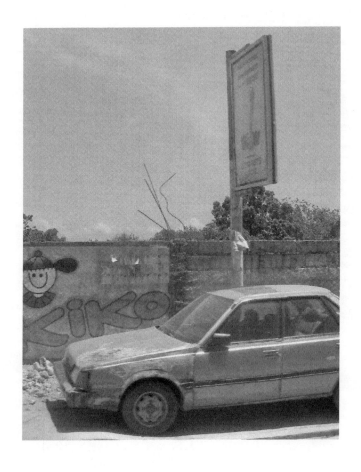

Chapter 10: Gason Lame (Army Men)

Morning came, and we had a fast breakfast of eggs, toast, and juice. John was dressed as casually as I'd ever seen him. He wore the outfit of your typical nondescript Haitian man who might be ambling around the streets of any city for lack of something meaningful to do. Esther was dressed similarly, in a long-skirt and a very conservative blouse with flat shoes. I was Peter Jensen, minus the beard, wearing my own pants but the Global Comms shirt and hat. Today's vehicle was a beat-up looking sedan not likely to draw the attention of anyone, and I sat in the back.

We made our way towards Port-au-Prince again, with John making endless turns he didn't need to. I thought at first that was so I couldn't remember any of our routes, but I think it was also just their standard operating procedure. The conversation was minimal, but the part I recall was John saying, *"I promised you a sidearm. You'll find in your tool bag a 9mm pistol. The safety is on, and there is a round in the chamber with a full magazine. That pistol stays in the bag unless the situation explodes and you are facing certain death. You will still be killed along with the rest of us, Mister Howard, but I don't believe in letting good men and woman be slaughtered without the dignity of fighting back."* Nina looked at me uncomfortably, with a sadness that I could feel.

We headed past the airport just a bit and promptly drove into the seventh circle of Hell- an immense shanty town slum called Cite Soleil. This was one of those few specific places listed on the State Department warnings... *"Don't come to Haiti, you stupid bastard. But if you DO come to Haiti, absolutely don't go to Cite Soleil. And if you DO go to Cite Soleil, you won't be leaving in one piece."* Yet, here I was, a stupid bastard rolling into Cite Soleil. Mercifully, this area with hundreds of thousands of the poorest souls in the Western Hemisphere was mostly spared by the devastating earthquake, although their already-shitty power grid feeds were made even more erratic in the tragedy. This was gang-turf, and just a few years prior there had been a bloody battle between UN stabilization troops and a few gangs right here, in the very garden spot where I was going to work.

Maybe an eighth of a mile in, the car was suddenly surrounded by grim looking men with more weapons than a National Guard unit. John rolled down the window, a few words were exchanged, and the men walked slowly besides the car as we made our way to a little blue cement building with no markings on it. This was our job site. Nina got out of the car and walked into the building while John and I waited. He spoke.

"These men are from the gang Gason Lame, which means Army Men. We have contracted with them to keep the Internet Café we are about to start in one of

their buildings free for all to use. We will have two connections- one for the people, and one for the gang. There is no other Internet availability anywhere here. Their leader understands that the Internet connection from NATCOM for the people is monitored, and if we find that the gang is abusing it at the expense of the people, we will sever the connection and minimally destroy their building..."

This was certainly different than doing networking back on the McDermott campus.

Esther stepped out, and motioned for us to come in. For this project, we had a couple of boxes in the back seat full of what we figured we needed. I brought a box and my tool bag, John brought the other box. The Gason Lame men said nothing but did kind of a lazy patrol around the building with one man staying next to our car. There were other people around outside of shacks down the streets, and most of them stared at us while we were going into the building.

Inside, Esther introduced me to Stanley. He was a big man who would have looked at home out with the tough guys guarding our perimeter. Stanley was very respectful despite his limited English skills. There was a lot of nodding, a few smiles, and a lot of Esther translating. There were two old wooden tables, one each on opposite walls in a room that was maybe ten feet by twelve. On each table was a brand-new Dell computer, monitor, mouse and keyboard. I can't imagine where they came from, and I did not ask.

That simple room was the makings of the new Internet cafe. In the small back room was another new computer for the gang's use and an enormous cabinet on the wall where the NATCOM fiber optic cable came into the building for the Internet connection, from a royal tangle of wires up on a nearby pole. There was new barbed wire around the bottom of the pole, because for various reasons cutting wires was a popular activity in Haiti. Esther and John started stretching out long patch cables that would be duct-taped to the walls between each computer and the small router appliance I was getting ready to configure in the back room with a laptop provided by Esther.

Suddenly the room went dark. I assumed that we were in one of Haiti's frequent power interruptions. I couldn't do much except help John and Esther run the wires and get them secured. Once that was done, we were at the mercy of the power situation before I could configure the router. John made it clear to me in English and to Stanley in French that we needed to get this done soon. The Gason Lame leader gave us a couple-hour window where our safety was "guaranteed", then we'd need to leave and not come back. We were a solid hour into that window.

Stanley and Esther were just about shouting at each other in French about something, when John intervened by slamming his hand on the table and saying something in French that obviously made Stanley pretty upset. After a short, uncomfortable silence Esther took John's cell phone, said something to Stanley in a low, angry voice, and handed the phone to him. Stanley spoke to someone, and suddenly we had power again. I'd learn later that we were being shaken down for money to keep the power on while we worked. John ended it with the promise the gang's leadership being arrested, and the building we were working in being destroyed by day's end. It wasn't a threat, but a statement of fact from a group that could and would make it happen.

As I configured the router to function as per Esther's instructions for the simple network we'd be leaving for public use, she wrote everything down neatly while explaining it to Stanley. They were friendly again, despite the tension only minutes ago. When I was done, it was time to test the computers. I went to see how one behaved, but John intercepted me. *"we'll take care of the testing, my friend. Please don't be offended. It would be best if you didn't have Internet access."* I could live with that.

They made sure that each computer could simply get out by testing random web sites. There would be no login required, and I had to significantly rate-limit each workstation in the router so no one of them could overwhelm the small Internet connection. Everything worked well, and Stanley was clearly very happy. Esther read me the rules in French that Stanley had taped on the wall for those who would use this new facility- no more than thirty minutes at time, no food or drink at the computers, any arguing about the rules would result in a lifetime ban, enforced by Stanley and ultimately the Gason Lame for as long as they were in control of this part of Cite Soleil. It all felt tenuous at best, but Esther explained to me that this would be small oasis of hope in one of the worst areas of Haiti. If it succeeded in getting poor people connected to the rest of the world for even a few months, the goal was that other Internet cafés might eventually be set up with gang help, if necessary- as long as the gang leaders benefitted as well there might be interest. I sensed that she was wasn't tremendously hopeful, but I understood that they needed to try.

Stanley sat down to do Windows updates, which would likely take days to complete for all the machines given the slow connection speed and the fact that the computers had been sitting somewhere for probably many months. But something was certainly better than nothing when you have nothing, and we had created a very nice little environment. There was a quick beep of a horn, and John said we needed to wrap up and get out. I told Esther that they should back up the router configuration in case they ever needed to replace it, and she said she'd tell Stanley how to do it over the phone at some point. I grabbed the tool bag and went to leave, and Stanley stepped directly in front of me. It was a little unnerving, but I noticed the big man had tears in his eyes. He gave me a quick hug, and in his best English said *"Thank you. Stanley thanks you and Cite Soleil thanks you."* John hustled me out, and we hit the road.

Esther took the tool bag with the gun up front with her. There was very little traffic getting out of Cite Soleil, which was almost as unnerving as being in the traffic jams. As we got close to the border of the slums, two motorcycles came up very fast behind us from out of nowhere. John told me to get down as low as I could as he and Esther both held pistols down next to their legs. The bikes came up beside either side of the car briefly, then fell back.

John told me it was OK to get up. *"They were our men."*

We made our way back to the house, and Esther decided that she wanted to configure the next router and do a configuration backup while I made sure she got it right. Her goal was to get more of the same routers to standardize on, to have spares and the ability to quickly get more Internet cafes popped up as opportunities arose. The hardest part would be the Internet connections, but they had people inside NATCOM and also had some Hughes satellite equipment and subscriptions they could deploy where fiber was not possible. The Internet café thing was a big deal, given how few Haitians at the time had any contact with the outside world. The general idea was that even limited exposure to the news and information from beyond Haiti would give people hope and reduce the feeling of isolation. It would also give them something to take pride in. The relationship with Gason Lame was an experiment at best, but I respected John and Esther for giving it a go.

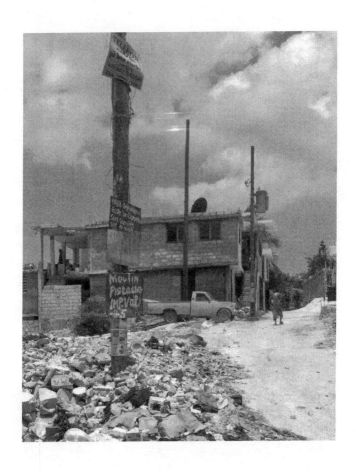

Chapter 11: Up and Away to Hinche

The rest of the day was spent talking shop with Esther about the next day's project, and then just hanging out- for me at least. We'd be setting up a wireless-only hotspot with a router, a small switch, and a couple of wireless access points. I wasn't sure where or for who yet. I suggested that we should get it all configured at the house before traveling, and to verify that it all worked in the relaxed environment of the house, rather than wait to do it onsite this time. Esther liked the sound of that, and she wanted to try it all herself "in the workshop", which I would never see. After we got to the point in the conversation where she felt comfortable getting started, Esther disappeared. I was on the balcony by myself for a while again.

My head hadn't been hurting much at all for the last day, and I was happy for that. The gash from the rock attack was healing, and I was getting used to not having hair on my head. Stubble was just starting to come back, and it reminded me of the mandatory head shave I endured back in Air Force basic training. I got through that, and I'd get through this. My broken tooth would eventually need repair, but all in all, it was looking like I'd generally be OK at the end of this odyssey- which John promised was coming soon. I trusted him, despite the oddness of the situation.

Now that I knew there was an end game, I was relaxing a bit and trying to enjoy the strange circumstances I was in. These were fundamentally good people, I had decided. I'd *never* understand much of Haiti's daily drumbeat, but goddam would I have stories to tell about it all someday.

I was looking out over my now-familiar view and taking it all in. My mind was all over the place, but I was also trying to stay grounded. I was in fact helping Haiti, just like the McDermott folks were hoping would happen- even if it wasn't the way it was supposed to get done. I was also sure that the things I was doing with John and Esther would be more impactful for Haitians than whatever we might have done with UAH. I sipped on a bottled water, and soon Nina came out to join me.

She brought an ice-cold Prestige, which we split, and man it tasted good. Nina told me how the Prestige brewery was founded in 1976, and that when she was a girl, one of her older brothers was a manager there. Her family was very proud. I asked if he had retired this many years later, and she quietly said *"Maynard was killed in the earthquake. His whole family was killed."* I looked at her as she stared down the hill. There were no tears in her eyes as I'm guessing they had all been cried out, but I found myself wanting to tear up a bit as I looked at her. All I could say was "I'm sorry, Nina". She smiled at me and said she had to go help with dinner.

The fucking place was so depressing.

The food, however, was always nice. It was like being kidnapped by Rachel Ray and Guy Fieri in that regard. That night we had a dish of chicken, rice, and diced vegetables all sauced up in something crazy delicious, but the highlight was being invited to have a glass of *rhum*. Nina explained that regular rum is derived from molasses, but rhum comes from the juice of sugarcane. This stuff was distilled in Haiti from some long-running company, and it was very nice indeed. I had a small glass straight, then a little bit in a makeshift punch that Esther made. Both were not quite like anything I had drank before in all my travels. After dinner, I conversationally helped Esther with just a couple of little configuration things that she was stuck on ahead of our next outing. She went to finish that all up, and John said he had to take care of business somewhere else that evening. I went back to my balcony to watch the evening take root over Port-au-Prince, and I fell asleep out there.

Around three in the morning, I was woken by a light rain when the wind pushed it just right at me on the balcony. I kind of just let the drops hit me, and I listened to the night sounds of the high-altitude neighborhood for maybe fifteen minutes. Then the rain picked up. I went back inside, and I was surprised to find a CD player and headphones on the bed. The disc had "Junior" written on it, and nothing else.

Was this meant to be entertainment, like as a gesture of kindness? Was Junior someone I was supposed to give two figs about? I laid down in the bed and put the phones on and turned on the player. There were thirteen tracks, and I just pressed play so start the first one. This was rap music, and I've never been a fan. But at the same time, it had a reggae kind of sway to it and the singer's voice was unique. It was interesting, but I was tired. I didn't get all the lyrics clear as I fell back asleep, but the chorus kinda stuck with me:

All a my brothers
All a my sisters
All a my lovers
Misses and misters
All gone away
Earth brake and sway
Will see you again
In heaven one day

It was heartfelt for sure. It was sad. But like so many things in Haiti, it was tinged with enough hope to sustain itself against its own weight. I'd eventually learn why I was supposed to listen to Junior, but his music was okay to my sleepy mind that night and back to slumberland I went.

A few hours later I was woken up by another mysterious person in my room. Strangely, I had gotten used to that odd ritual. This time it was a Canadian man in a fight suit with captain's rank and aviator glasses. I was still groggy, but I took a shot. "Good morning, John."

"Am I that obvious, Mister Howard? You are not fooled by Captain Adrian Sinclair of the Royal Canadian Air Force? I need to step up my game. Maybe I should try being a white man sometime…" That seemed to amuse him greatly. I said if anyone could do it, it would be him. But why the flight suit?

"Because we'll be flying, of course."

All right then.

After breakfast, I was Peter Jensen once more. This time, Esther was also a Global Comms employee, complete with shirt and ID. We ended up back in the UN vehicle and headed for the airport area again with the equipment we'd need for wherever we were going. John and Esther were in a great mood, and there didn't seem to be any of the gloom that travelled with us to Cite Soleil just the day before. Was it just yesterday? I guess it was, the events tended to just blur together there.

We did the usual semi-random zig-zaggy route towards the city, and as we got close to the airport perimeter John's phone rang. He had it on speaker so Esther could also hear. There was great worry in the conversation that I could not understand because of the language. After the call ended, John pulled over and spoke, looking back me. *"We will have to go through a checkpoint to get to our helicopter. But it is not real police involved. It may turn violent... there are only two men and we will be fine. Please just stay quiet and do not leave the vehicle for any reason, Howard."*

Ah, geeze. Here we go again.

To get to where we needed to be, we had to take a service road into a part of the airport that sat well away from where the commercial airline operations went on. There was only one way in, and fences and drainage ditches didn't allow for driving off the pavement. I could see the road ahead blocked by a motorcycle, with a truck next to the road. Neither had any real markings. Beyond, maybe the length of a football field, sat a couple of helicopters. As we approached, a man in police uniform with a large automatic rifle stepped into the road and motioned us to stop. The other man took a position on the passenger side. John rolled up to them and brought his window half down. There was brief conversation in French as both fake policemen tried to look into the back seat and cargo area. The other man knocked on the window, telling Esther to roll it down. She ignored him. Whatever John said to his guy led to the man outside the driver's side raising his voice. John rolled the window down the rest of the way, then things got hot. The man on the passenger side fell hard against the Range Rover, he had clearly been shot in the head. He kinda lingered upright for a few seconds before falling to the ground. John's guy looked up to see what happened to his partner, and

John fired off three shots in quick succession into him all in the area of the heart. It was over in seconds. *"Stay put back there, Mister Howard. It's over, but stay put."* John said calmly.

He and Esther both got out, and quickly gathered the dead men's weapons and wallets and whatever else was in their pockets and in the truck and put it all in the back of our vehicle. John moved the motorcycle aside and knifed both of its tires. He took the key from the motorcycle and the truck and shot two of the truck tires and put one round straight into the radiator. The men were left where they fell. John put a fresh clip in his pistol, took another look around, then got back into the vehicle. Esther made a phone call, and while she did, John asked if I was OK. I certainly was, though I was blown away that all of this just happened and there were no sirens. Nobody was coming to check it out. In a city that has far too many people, no one was around to see what just happened on the sprawling airport grounds. John told me that those men were two of the worst of the worst among local criminals, and had been involved with kidnap, murder, and other crimes against both foreigners and Haitians. We drove forward toward the helicopters.

John pulled up next to a Bell Kiowa with Canadian Air Force markings. There was another man in a flight suit waiting, and he had an automatic rifle with a scope on it. That explained who shot the passenger-side fake policeman. He also wore a captain's rank, and he was perhaps the largest man I had ever seen in

Haiti. Both tall and extremely muscular, John introduced me to our pilot Dominique. Esther gave him a quick kiss on the cheek. We got the equipment loaded along with the guns taken from the dead men, and John went to move the vehicle into the small hangar building nearby.

As I was getting in the helicopter, I noticed fancy black letters against the black paint of the aircraft. All the military markings were in white, aside from the Canadian flag emblem, but the words *Unpainted Whore* were clearly spelled out in a black-on-black scrolling font. I was trying to recall where I had heard that phrase, and Dominique saw me looking at it. *"Slaughterhouse Five, Kurt Vonnegut- you are familiar?"*, he asked, smiling. I said I was, I had read it a couple of times through the years. In his accent he said *"I am a big fan. I have all Vonnegut books. And so I named the aircraft. I also have a truck I call Billy Pilgrim."* Dominique seemed downright proud. Why the hell not? It made as much sense as anything else in Haiti. I liked his spirit.

John sat up front with Dominique, Esther and I were in the back, and we all had headphones to talk above the noise. I heard someone on the ground calling for "Canadian Air Force helo, please acknowledge" a couple of times as we took off. It sounded like maybe the American military was doing air traffic control duty from someplace not obvious given that the tower itself looked pretty rough with quake damage. John explained that we would just ignore them and the

104

assumption would be that a wrong frequency was in use in the chaos of all the various governments operating in Haiti. We certainly were not the Canadian Air Force despite the aircraft markings and uniforms, and so better to have no conversations.

It was astounding to see the building ruins from the air, to see just what a terrible hand the earth itself had dealt to the residents on the ground during the quake. It was obvious that building codes were not a high priority in Haiti, and it was horrific to think of people trapped under the endless slabs of concrete and piles of debris that were buildings not so long ago. I couldn't help but think of the two guys that were just killed on the road. They survived the quake only to make life miserable for others. *Karma, bitches.* I could muster no sympathy for them.

John told me a few minutes into the flight then we were on our way to the town of Hinche, about a forty-five minute flight northwest of Port-au-Prince. Hinche survived the quake largely intact but got its share of refugees from Port-au-Prince who had no place to go. The road into Hinche was currently an impassible mud pit, so we were going in by air.

Some NGO had found a way to get a couple dozen laptops from the One Laptop per Child initiative in Africa diverted into Hinche, and we'd be setting up a place where adults and children alike could use those devices for a range of purposes. Again my mind went back to the two dead men, and to John. The more time I spent with John and his crew, the more he felt like something akin to a super-hero crossed with a saint. And the more I hated those who attacked me in the street, and all the others who are behind those terrifying State Department warnings.

As we flew over the hills and forests and roads, every now and then Dominque would point out something he thought I might find interesting. *"Look down to the left, Mister Howard- there is a beautiful waterfall..."* I watched Esther working dutifully away in a notebook, and I noticed a sticker on the cover that showed a young man singing with the name "Ekselan Junior" in bold lettering underneath his image. I learned that in Haiti, there are no coincidences. When the radio chatter was quiet, I asked Esther over the headphones about who had given me the CD player and the Junior disc as I pointed at her notebook. Her head spun towards me fast, and before she could answer, Dominque was singing over the headset *"All a my brothers, all a my sisters, all a my lovers..."* Esther playfully told him to shut up. They obviously had some kind of relationship. John chimed in and said *"I thought you should like to hear Ekselan Junior. His real name is Junior Vincent, and he's quite the young man. He is a native son of Haiti and he sells quite well internationally. Ekselan means Excellent in Creole. Nina actually gave him his stage name, but that is a long story. You'll be meeting him, Mister Howard."* I didn't get a chance to ask what that was about, as Dominique started the decent into Hinche.

We landed in an open field, where a van was waiting for us. I was surprised to see an older white woman standing beside it. She was introduced as Ruth, and I was Peter Jensen to her. When she heard the name, she glanced quick at John and then back at me. Ruth had a thick British accent, and she helped us to unload the gear from the helicopter. I was surprised when she picked up the dead men's guns and wallets and put them in the van, with no comment or question whatsoever. Evidently, she had been told about the goings on back at the airport and was somehow in the group's circle if she was handling dead men's weapons as if she was simply taking a bag of laundry out of the car. We made our way maybe fifteen minutes from the field to a small compound, where Ruth dropped John and Dominique off. They had some sort of business in town and would be changing clothes and using a vehicle from a few that were parked nearby. Ruth, Esther and I drove on just a bit to the building where we'd do our work.

We came in on a private drive behind the structure but were now looking at the street-facing side of things. The building was half concrete and half wood, with a very large, corrugated metal-covered patio. We'd be putting two wireless access points under the patio, and I noticed that someone had already strategically installed electrical outlets on four support poles for keeping the laptops charged. We'd need to run a couple of network wires from the patio to the inside of the building, where a network area had been set up. Another enormous NATCOM fiber cabinet where the Internet came in dwarfed the small shelf where our router would go. Esther had already done the router and access point configuration work back at the house, and she got things physically situated inside while I ran the wires and made the connections. Ruth would be the caretaker and administrator of the simple network and she was very business-like as she asked both Esther and I all sorts of questions about how it would all work. The ladder I had to use was pretty shoddy, and I didn't feel very safe on it at all. I saw a small crowd of kids watching from the street intently through fence bars. I motioned for one young man to come in, but three others followed. Despite the language barrier, I got them to hold the ladder steady for me. Those kids held onto that ladder with great pride and seriousness. There were just a handful of screws to put into the wooden beams for holding things up, and I let each one of the boys go up the ladder and screw one in by hand with a screwdriver. As each finished, they came down the ladder with huge smiles. That greatly pleased Ruth, and she gave them each some candy as a thank-you.

The work went quickly- like maybe two hours total. Ruth and Esther did all the testing. After the verification that things were in operational order, Ruth made sure all the laptops were locked up in a chain-link fenced area until their first use. I got the impression that these cheap laptops were as valuable as gold to that crowd. We sat down under the metal roof and had bottled water, but there wasn't a lot of conversation. Pretty much each of us knew that our circumstances didn't let us get to know each other any better, but we were simply content to be on the same team for a little while. Ruth said she was from Cornwall, but that is all I would learn about her. To this day she is one more of Haiti's mystery's to me.

Before too long, Dominique and John came back. They were carrying a couple of bags of lunch. Somewhere they found *griot*- fried pork chunks, and macaroni salad like none I'd ever had before. It was all in neat foil packages that made for a nice picnic. The salad was rich with diced vegetables and maybe perhaps a little too much vinegar, which was just delicious against the saltiness of the pork chunks. We ate while Esther made sure Ruth had a handle on the small network. Afterwards, John and Dominique put their flight suits back on. We put our tools back in the helicopter, and I was curious about what would become of those guns that Ruth seemed to have no problem handling but it really wasn't anything I could ask about. Quick goodbyes were said, and I didn't realize until we were in the air that Ruth had said "goodbye *Howard*". We headed back into the sky.

As we got close to Port-au-Prince, I noticed that we weren't getting any lower. John told us all that we had a quick stop to make on Gonave, the big island that sat in the Gulf out in front of the city a few dozen miles. We flew low over the ocean, almost like Dominique and John were looking either for or at something, or possibly staying under radar level. I tried to just take in what I could see as I knew my time there was growing shorter and it was hard not to somewhat enjoy the unique tour I was getting. We put down on a dirt airstrip, and I could see a small group of armed men standing around a white man in handcuffs. There was some chatter on the radio in French and then Esther looked at me sadly. She pulled the black bag out and handed it me and apologized. As I put it on, I took one last look outside and saw the man in cuffs getting a needle put in his arm. Though I couldn't see, after that I have no doubt that the man was loaded onto the helicopter from what I could hear. It happened so fast that Dominique didn't even kill the engine. We flew back to Port-au-Prince in silence, and Esther asked me to stay covered after the engine was shut down. Dominique grabbed my hand and said it was nice to meet, and then I heard a vehicle leave. John said I could uncover, then their was just Esther and John again. He looked at me and asked, *"are you hanging in there, Mister Howard?"* I was, but my head was also hurting a bit for the first time in a day and a half. I looked over at where the bogus roadblock was this morning, and there was no sign that it ever existed except for a prominent bloodstain on the pavement. When we headed back to the house, I fell asleep in the Range Rover.

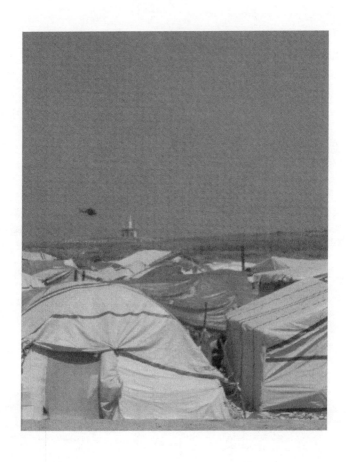

Chapter 12: A Brush with Fame

At dinner that night, John apologized to me for what I had to see that day with the two men killed. But he was emphatic that they had absolutely been behind a number of terrible crimes, and that Haiti and all who visit her would be better for their passing. I assured him that I understood. Sometimes instant justice is the best, I've always felt even if that runs contrary to the rules of civilization. I asked about the fellow from the island. Nina said very point-blank that he would be a "guest" in another house. He was a South African drug smuggler and human trafficker. The Haitian police were not interested in apprehending him because of "connections to government officials". He might be returned for a hefty fee to whatever group would claim such a man, or he might simply disappear. It all came down to what they got back on him from their research.

John also said that we had a slight change of plans to the coming day. Our third and last network project would have to wait a day, because something else had come up. We would deal with the "special circumstance", as John put it, tomorrow, instead of when our three network projects were done. Then the following day we'd take care of our last project- and I would also be sent on my way home directly from that final location.

I let that sink in, and it felt weird.

No one at the table spoke for a little bit, and I had no real idea what to say. I raised my water bottle and without really thinking I said "to all of you." They raised their various drinks, and then it was silent again. Finally, Nina spoke, asking me if I'd like either a beer or a rhum punch. I answered "after the day's events, I'd actually like both, to be honest." John simply nodded, and pretty soon I had both drinks in front of me. I was rather foggy in the noggin for some reason, and alcohol couldn't make it any worse, I figured.

Nina looked directly at me, but she was speaking in French to John. As Nina and Esther picked up the dishes, John took a deep breath and looked at me. *"This might seem somewhat strange, Howard, but tomorrow we go someplace... special. I need to ask that you free your mind..."* He smiled a little.

"Ekselan Junior is trying to cut a new album, but the network or something in his studio keeps acting up. He's very cutting edge by standards in Haiti, and his main technical man was badly injured in a protest and is in hospital. Esther has tried to troubleshoot, but it's a very strange problem and we're hoping you might help. He has a contractual deadline that is approaching fast, and we are- well, he is- somewhat desperate. There are no other studios for him to work in right now, at least not that would be practical and safe."

114

I said fine, whatever it took- but I did remind them all that I'm not a sound engineer and Esther may have already looked at anything I might think of for the problem. My mind was processing that I was actually in my last couple of days in Haiti, and there was light at the end of my tunnel. It had been maybe a week and a couple of days so far, but it felt like months. Now there was a rap artist that needed my help. You couldn't make this shit up if you tried.

Nina gifted me another Prestige, and I went to my balcony to sip it, to watch the night fall, and to listen to some Ekselan Junior. There was an incredible fog over Port-au-Prince that evening, and we were kind of right at the underbelly of the clouds where the house was located. It was really beautiful in a sort of morose way that went well with my mood after that roller coaster ride of a day. It felt like if I reached out over the balcony, I might be able to touch a big sad cloud. I drained the beer and settled into the music. I found that I loved the reggae behind the rap, and every now and then that fast rap beat kind of transitioned away from the autotuning and computer processing and into Junior's clear, pure voice- almost ballad-like. The dude could really sing. He truly was *ekselan*.

I had about an hour to myself, and I needed it after the day's various stimuli. I was listening to a song called *The Devil's Tap-Tap* and zoning out when I noticed that Esther was waiting for me to see her in the doorway. I took off the earphones, and she came out with a small MP3 player and a little speaker attached to the headphone jack. She also asked if I wanted another rhum punch or a beer, and again I said I'd have both if possible. I needed it. She looked at me maybe a bit worried, and I promised her I wasn't an alcoholic and that didn't usually drink that much. It had just been a hell of a day and a hell of a week in a hell of a place. She called Nina on her phone, and pretty soon I had that tropical rhum goodness in my hand. If you gotta get kidnapped in Haiti, I can't recommend finding this group strongly enough.

Esther said *"This is Junior's latest music and the problem that we are trying to solve. You'll hear the issue about midway through this song, just a terrible noise. It's worse in other songs, sometimes it's just a little and sometimes it's overwhelming..."* She hit play, and the little speaker was surprisingly clear. Junior was singing a song about young men needing to make a choice between right and wrong, the backing track was just awesome. Right as he got to the chorus:

> *Island boy gonna be an island man*
> *Gotta decide where you stand*
> *So easy to take the dirty road down*
> *But we need more good men in this town*
> *What's it gonna be Island Man?*
> *What's it gonna BE Island Man?*

The vocals went to hell just then. It sounded like an old cassette tape that had gotten twisted and damaged but still somehow played. Esther said they were having trouble filtering it out and it was very intermittent. Their studio tech guy Jimmy in the hospital couldn't talk or even write things on paper from his injuries, and they didn't know where to start troubleshooting. There was a lot of wireless technology in use and no wired connections available to try instead. Some of it was networked and some of it not. Esther played a couple of other examples. All sounded similar- mostly clear, then it went in the toilet. She asked if I had any ideas, with her notebook in hand.

I told her that without knowing anything about the environment, I'd start by trying to pin down when the trouble was first noticed. Was any new equipment introduced, either in the studio or in any adjacent rooms? They said there was a lot of wireless stuff in play, so there was a chance something outside of the studio could be a problem. I suggested that we figure out *everything* that was wireless in the studio and outside rooms and what frequency and channel each was using if we could. One of Esther's police scanners could maybe help here, as it had frequency counter and nearby signal detection features. She was pleased with all of this, and then offered up her own thought- *"Could a faulty electrical circuit contribute if something in the studio was plugged into it?"* I didn't know how if that was possible, but Esther might have been on to something else without realizing it.

117

A lot of those cheap AC-to-DC power transformer devices that come with various equipment, and even laptop computer power supplies, could generate noise if they were faulty or not shielded right in the construction process. Esther said that they hadn't really considered any of this, and so she was hopeful. I didn't want to burst her bubble and say that whatever equipment was being used also might just be faulty, because then we probably couldn't do much to fix it or find replacements very fast on the island.

Nina and John came by my balcony hangout, and Esther shared what we were talking about with them. Everyone seemed optimistic, and I was happy for that, but I also hoped the expectation for success hadn't been raised too much. I knew that even if we couldn't solve Junior's problems, Esther would be better at her various tasks going forward for the experience so at least there would be a silver lining. Junior's defective music played on, and pretty soon Nina and Esther were dancing a little and talking about something that was making them laugh a lot, and John offered me a cigarette. Again I took it, despite not being a smoker. He and I stared out into the valley, two men of action puffing on smokes after a hard day of networking and killing our fellow man, while the ladies swayed off to our right.

I really liked these people. I know I've said it a couple of times, but it's gotta come out. They were my captors, yet I appreciated what more there was to each of them. I still have great fondness for the trio this long after the fact, and there is no Stockholm Syndrome or whatever in play by my own analysis. They just felt like intrinsically good humans on the right side of a lot of fucked up situations, functioning well together as a team. They could be barbaric when that was called for, but they could be generous and sweet and at the core they were just *good*. They left their marks on me, each of them as I recall my time there.

By the time the night wound down, I had a decent buzz going. I'm not a recreational drinker, but I really did appreciate the altered state at that particular point. I'm pretty adaptable to people and situations and consider myself cool "under fire" in that expressions' various connotations, but I was also maybe pushing my limit of sanity after being grabbed up by my new colleagues and walking around with a bruised brain.

The next day brought delicious oatmeal, fruit, and toast for breakfast. And mango juice- which was the best I have ever had anywhere. Nina gave me a vitamin and an aspirin, predicting a hangover that thankfully did not materialize. There were no uniforms or costumes this go round, but John told me to please continue to "be" Peter Jensen. Evidently Ekselan Junior and this group were tight, and there was a low-grade excitement about the outing at hand that I could feel. John, Nina, and Esther all went this time, and we made the trip in the same beater sedan we had taken to Cite Soleil. Once we got to whatever the magic spot was, I could feel Nina pulling the black bag off of my head. I thanked her, and she looked awkward. I don't want to say that we were friends by then, but there was at least an element of that in play. There was basic comfort and respect, for sure. And we enjoyed talking with each other as professional equals.

Junior lived in one of those magnificent houses high above Petion-ville. We rolled up to the gate, and I noticed the top part was fabricated as the ledger lines like on sheet music, with several notes playfully splashed across. Without realizing I had said it, "kinda like Graceland" came out of my mouth and Nina said that Junior was a big Elvis fan, like his father had been. John made a call, and soon the gate opened for us and closed once the car was in.

We drove to the front of what I would call a mansion, and this house would be easy to appreciate in any country. As we were getting out, the big front door opened, and there stood *Ekselan Junior*. I was surprised at what I saw. I had expected a stereotypically dressed rapper like out of American videos- gold chains, flashy clothes, sunglasses- but this gentleman was dressed more like he was going to the golf course. Polo shirt, khakis, big nerd glasses, and no jewelry or tattoos that I could see. One by one, my travel companions hugged him and quick stories were exchanged. Then Junior looked at me and said *"Mr. Jensen, thank you so much for coming. I share in my friends' sadness for your circumstances here in*

Haiti, and you have my gratitude for all you've done for us. Please, come into my home."

I thanked him and told him to please call me Peter. John chuckled at that. I took Junior's greeting to mean that the singer was also part of whatever this mysterious group was. By then, nothing surprised me anymore. Nothing- and everything- made sense.

Junior, John, and Nina had business somewhere else in the house. Esther told Junior that she and I were going to the studio, and that we might have to look around at a few other rooms at his various wireless gadgets. He said *"Whatever you need, my dear, you know your way around. I'll be with you soon."* The studio was impressive, at least to me. It wasn't huge, but it was spotless and looked very contemporary. I had no idea what almost any of the gadgetry was, but it was neat to think that this digital sausage grinder was where the music I had listened to came from. I noticed that beyond the studio there was a swimming pool outside, with tennis courts nearby. Various trees and shrubs gave privacy from whatever neighbors might be beyond the grounds, which was a striking contrast to the elbow-to-elbow way people were squeezed in down the hill. Junior was living large.

Esther and I dug right in; we made a list of everything we could find that was wireless, looking for frequency conflicts. Eventually everyone was in on it. There were a few potential competing devices in the mix, but nothing stood out as a slam-dunk answer to the issue. I asked Junior if he could try to recreate the conditions and workflow that resulted in the odd noise getting sucked into the song and processing software. That took a little doing, but he got everything set up. He generally worked between two microphones for his vocals, with one in the mixing booth and one in the studio he shared with his backup singers when they all recorded together. Most of the time he was right in the booth though, as he loved to fidget with the sound board, synthesizer, auto tuner, and whatever else was in there. He would stand or sit and sing as he manipulated various sliders. We talked through the fact that the problem didn't seem related to any one piece of equipment based on when it occurred.

We decided to do an experiment. Junior put on a backing track and handed Nina, Esther, and John some lyrics to follow along with and to exercise the backup mics while he did his thing out in front. We'd see if we could replicate the offensive sound. They all got into singing the song and were having great fun, but Junior was listening close for the trouble to surface, and I was watching him monkey around with his controls. Just as he got into a solo verse, he pressed the computer keyboard- and that weird noise came through. Everyone stopped. Junior said *"That was it! That's what we're trying to find!"*

I pointed out that he had just pressed the keyboard, as I saw it. Something had to have come from that. Junior was skeptical- it was a very expensive

Bluetooth keyboard that he got from a recent trip to Korea. I asked him if he had the problem before that keyboard was introduced. He didn't answer, but his wheels were turning. From a shelf he took his old keyboard, and paired it to the PC after turning off the fancy Korean one. *"Sing for me again my friends, let's see if Mister Peter has found our needle in the haystack."*

On the second take, Junior hit the keyboard and there was no noise created.

There was great relief and happiness that we had indeed found the problem. We also went down the list of other things to watch out for in the future, like cheap power supplies and any other new gadget introduced. I gave Esther a couple of ideas on inexpensive spectrum analyzers and companion software to think about, as that would be the best tool for this sort of thing. We had done what we came to do, and Junior broke out a bottle of good California wine to celebrate. It was the only time I saw John take a drink, and then it was just to be polite as Junior toasted the end of the "sound curse", as he described it. With hours left in the day, Junior suggested that we try to get a song recorded. *"I don't have my singers here, so you all will do me the honor…"* It seemed that they had history together- maybe they all grew up together, with Nina as an older sister to somebody here? They were so comfortable with each other, there had to be family connections or something close to it.

Junior wanted to try *Baby Got to Leave*, which eventually ended up making it onto his *Supreme Ekselan* disc the exact way we made it that day. He had the backing track all ready, and Nina, Esther and John were like little kids at their microphones. It was fun to watch, and a little odd to see John taking direction instead of giving it. Junior was in command, despite always smiling at his friends. He dug into the song:

> *My woman told me*
> *I ain't getting it done*
> *She needs a strong man,*
> *maybe I'm not the one*
> *Letting her down,*
> *letting me down,*
> *getting so down*
> *That girl deserves better,*
> *I got to fix what I've done*

It was bluesy and sad despite being up-tempo, and Junior put the right emotion where it needed to be. I could see why he was so popular because he was just a natural at his craft. When it got to the chorus and the background "*Baby got to leave, the girl's gonna go*" part, Junior wasn't happy with what he was getting out of John and the ladies. He said it needed something, then he looked at me. I felt like a little kid in school hoping that the teacher didn't call on me. But indeed, the request came.

"Mister Peter, I have a feeling that you may be the missing piece of my little puzzle. Can I impose on you? It's just a handful of words, repeated several times. Won't you give me a hand?"

What the hell. Why not? My odyssey in Haiti was already batshit strange, why not pile on a bit more guano? I said I'd do it, but I'd need some dark glasses so I could feel like a proper rapper. Junior chuckled, and went and found me some shades. Esther looked at me, I saluted her with my hip new look, and she busted out laughing. And I sang. I thought I sounded like bloody hell as my voice came out, but Junior was happy as a *kochon nan labou*. He played it back minus my voice, and then with my contribution so we could all hear the difference. It really did sound better with me in the mix. You gotta try stuff.

The song ended up doing quite well throughout the Caribbean when the disc was released a couple of moths after I left Haiti, and Junior was kind enough to send me an autographed copy of *Supreme Ekselan*. In the liner notes he included "a special thank you to Mr. Peter Jensen for his technical and vocal assistance". He's a class act, and for decades my background singing will be heard far and wide on the radio in the islands.

After we closed down the recording session, I sat out by the pool sipping an ice-cold Presidente beer.

Esther, John, and Junior were making us a late lunch, and Nina stayed with me. She told me that it was very nice that I helped Junior out that day, and that his sales helped their collective efforts and therefor I helped Haiti again in a big way. I told her that I was glad I could be of service even if I had no real choice in the matter, and even though I would never understand who they all were. She got pensive then.

"Soon you will leave us. You are not our typical guest. You are a good man, and I can only imagine that you'll think of us often in the months and years to come. The more you do, the more questions you will have that can never be answered. I apologize for that weight being given to you."

I answered without even really thinking first. "Nina, I was attacked, and your group saved me from bad people. You've fed me wonderful food, and you've given me company. It's been weird, but you figured out who I am and who I am not. I was never tied up or shackled or beaten although I know that you all are capable of that. You guys did fuck with my mind a little bit, and yesterday I watched John kill a man that I could have reached out and touched. Now today I'm a backup singer recording in a studio in a mansion. Yes, I will think about you all often- whether I want to or not. I'm not so sure that I'll be asking myself questions about anything, but I know I'll never forget this strange outing. Whatever your group is, your mission and existence will be forever safe with me. I understand the gravity of what you all do even if I will never really understand Haiti. I can only hope there is a group like yours operating in the US somewhere."

Nina just stared at me. Her eyes were kind, and I know there is more that she'd like to have said but couldn't. Then the others came out with the most delicious looking pork sandwiches and beet salad. We feasted by the pool, although conversation stayed fairly surface given that I was still the outsider. It was fine. I thoroughly enjoyed the food, and I understood my circumstances. I had no complaints. The sky was getting kind of dark with rain clouds as we finished eating, and thunder was building up off above different hills over the city. We rapped up the meal just before the first drops fell.

After we ate, Junior gave me a tour of his home. He had a modest den of sorts with lots of professional accolades, and pictures of him with various American celebrities. He wasn't gaudy in how he showed his awards and accomplishments, and even in the pictures he had a humbleness about him. Junior was the real deal when it came to superstars, but he was gracious and reserved. I was really glad that I found his problem, if for no other reason than because he was a decent gent. So far, we knocked it outta the park with regards to John's to-do list here, in Cite Soleil, and in Hinche. My conditions release were strange and arguably exploitive, but I'd be lying if I said I didn't mostly enjoy the experiences.

We left Junior's, and instead of going up the hill back to the house, we headed down into Port-au-Prince so Esther could pick up something or other she needed for the next day's project. The rain was fierce, and the sky was pretty ugly where it should have been showing late afternoon daylight. John mentioned there was a tropical storm out to sea and we were getting the edges of that. I saw side streets fill up pretty quickly with water, carrying garbage and debris in multiple brand new rivers. Looking up at the endless tents and tiny pop-up shelters on the hillside, I could imagine horrific landslides taking place if too much rain found its way to those slopes. Everywhere my eyes wandered it seemed like I was looking at past tragedy, or trouble yet to come.

We stopped somewhere near the Iron Market, and Esther was back in the car in two minutes or less. We headed back up to our high ground, but we got bogged down a little in traffic at an intersection. As I looked out my window, I couldn't make sense of what was coming down the road at us until Nina screamed at John to hit the gas- a wall of plastic bottles was being driven by a flash flood directly at us. John was able to get us out of there, but I turned and watched the surge out the back window sweep across the intersection we just left. The wave was at least as tall as the car and laden with trash. If one thing in Haiti isn't trying to kill you, something else is right around the corner, biding its time.

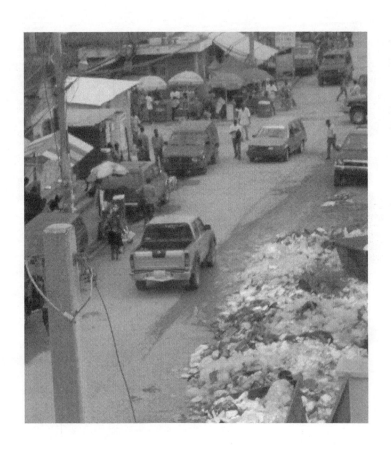

Chapter 13: Les Cayes- the Final Project

When we finally got back to the house, the heaviest rain was done. All the way back up the road, each one of John's, Nina's, and Esther's phones were beeping and ringing almost non-stop. Almost every call was in French, but I got the impression that the storm was creating havoc and these three were pivotal to getting response and relief where it was needed for many people in the area. Then I thought of Dominique. And Ruth. And even the gun guys out on Gonave, who handed over the drug dealer in cuffs. And maybe even Eksalan Junior. Were they all getting calls tonight? All coordinating help for people in parallel with whatever the local governments might be doing? Or did maybe this shadowy group actually work with local governments, and not compete with them? Maybe there was permutations of all of that, but I do know that the two women and the one man in that car with me were absolutely devoted to serving Haiti. It was just hard to fathom where all the connections might be made in the big picture.

Dinner that night had a bit of a festive feel. John did point out that it was our last supper together, but he said we'd talk about the specifics of my leaving later on. We had more joumou- that delicious pumpkin soup. But most impressive was the gigantic, whole fish that was shared by all of us. I don't remember what kind it was, but the presentation and the taste was incredible. On the side was the most exotic macaroni and cheese you could imagine, and my mouth waters just thinking back on it. I mostly skipped the beer and the rhum that last night and stuck with Coke, but I did have one rhum and Coke on the balcony after dinner.

The table talk was mostly about Ekselan Junior's various travels and successes. He was clearly a national treasure, and that he was recognized internationally was a bigger thing to this group than I could ever explain. I guess there was a feeling that there wasn't much that Haiti as a country could point to with pride at that point in time. We had *blan manje* for dessert alongside with fresh coffee. That struck me as fairly pudding-like, but maybe also a cousin of crème brulee, with strong coconut flavor. Just absolutely freaking delicious.

Finally, we got around to talking about the next day. We were on the balcony again. Like a good commander, John was in "need to know" mode until the end. He told me we'd be on the road for a few hours, possibly more if the night's heavy rain flooded out the highway where we were heading. I should take all of my belongings, and I should know that I'd be leaving by boat when we were done with our work. That's all he wanted to reveal that night, and he said the rest would come as we got closer to where we needed to be the next day. I was good with all that. Then John surprised me.

"Please listen to me now, Mister Howard. I have been in contact with our highest leaders about you. Not government, no... but those in our organization. Your case is unique, and you have our gratitude. I personally will miss you- you've grown on us here in this house. At the same time, it is a leap of faith that you will not leave us, and ultimately betray the secrecy of our organization even if not purposefully. I promised you some form of compensation, so let us talk about all of this."

I suddenly felt guilty, despite having done nothing wrong. I tried to tell John I had no interest in talking about his group at all. I told him to help me come up with a cover story, and I'd stick to it until I died. Then I got worried- do they not trust me? Could I end up dead over spending too much time with them? I was whimpering like a child, I suppose.

"Mister Howard, you are in no danger. Please let me get all of this said." John was about the most even-keel guy I think I've ever met, anywhere. *"Our existence is extremely well-known to those who NEED to know about it, those who we coordinate with both inside Haiti and beyond. To the general population, we are a mystery. Some say we are Haiti's hope in the worst of times, others think we are little more than a gang of thugs attached to the government. To most people we are like Santa Clause, just a fable. That mystique is an asset, but also a liability at times. Now back to you, Mister Howard- we would like you, as a foreigner, to help us*

to adjust our perception somewhat. When you get home, and when you are comfortable doing so, write a book about your time with us. Tell what you've seen, what you've experienced, but fictionalize it enough to not give any of us away. Change the names, the locations, but otherwise get your adventure on paper."

Um, maybe I could do that. I didn't fancy myself a book author, but I had done a fair amount of professional writing as part of my job. It probably wasn't that much of a stretch, and there was a good story to be told. But I asked John why- what was the goal?

"If such a book was written, especially by an outsider, we would buy thousands of copies and get it spread all around Haiti far and wide. The people would have hope that there are other forces besides corrupt politicians and questionable police keeping their country going. The gangs and common criminals will know that they might think twice about their activities. Even those corrupt members of our National Police might get just a little worried. Such a book will not change the world for Haiti as our problems run deep, but it might provide hope. From what I think I know of you. It would certainly entertain. And it would be something positive for our children to think about... to aspire to. I was once in a gang myself as very young man before I learned there was another path to follow. You would not believe the

extent of my training and education compliments of our organization. "

On this point, John was dead-wrong. After seeing him in action, I pictured John and Dominque training in Quantico or with Navy Seals or other top-notch agencies in the US or the like. There was real substance here that I would never know the underpinnings of, but I have no doubt that John had spent quality time training with anyone from the FBI to the Mossad.

I didn't really know what to say to the entire narrative. John just let me process it all. We both looked out over the valley and Port-au-Prince below. Then he continued to say that my compensation for this whole endeavor of the last week and a half would be guaranteed book sales in large quantities, and perhaps even an eventual movie deal with one of a couple of Haitian filmmakers. Book income was guaranteed, the movie idea was a twinkle in his eye (his words) but his leadership felt it was time to expose their organization just a little for the advancement of a number of goals, through the eyes of a foreigner. I was that foreigner. Just like in the beginning when I sensed something bad would eventually happen to me in Haiti, I also sensed at that moment that I would one day be doing the book thing. John's organization was giving me permission to talk about them, and they were also asking for my help- which I'd be happy to give when the timing was right for me.

I felt just a mild headache coming on, and John said his goodnights. The next morning would be the start of my last day in Haiti, and I had a lot to think about.

Breakfast brought an incredible Haitian spaghetti, rich in garlic and tomatoes with some fish thrown in for protein and flavor. Nina said we needed full bellies for the day ahead. When we were done, I said my goodbyes to Nina. I thanked her for everything, she thanked me for everything in return, then a nice hug was our last interaction, other than her giving my head stubble one last quick rub. I carried my small suitcase to the garage, and this time there was no black bag. I saw nothing but closed doors as we made our way down a couple of flights of stairs.

We had maybe a three-hour ride to Les Cayes, which was a port on the southern coast. We were in the UN sport utility again, and John was the Jamaican policeman UN guy. I was just me, no more Peter Jensen. We were headed to an interesting little complex, where different government agencies from several countries operated out of, in small boats, just down the coast a couple of miles from the beautiful Les Cayes beaches and commercial port operations.

We ended up taking a road that could barely be called that, and we needed the sport utility's muscle to get through some nasty mud from the previous day's rain. We ended up at an old cinder block building, and I noticed the wireless bridge connection pointing back towards town. There was no NATCOM fiber out to this little patch of jungle. There was a decent dock, and all of this was blocked from being seen from the city of Les Cayes by a bend of the coast. I couldn't imagine what we'd be doing here. Esther led us past this building to the front of a newly constructed smaller block building. It looked like a vault. I noticed generators next to each building, and a couple of radio antennas on a small tower mounted to the side of the larger building. There were also a couple of cameras on the new building, one pointed at the dock and one looking towards the front of the old building.

Then John told me what we were doing there. *"The bigger building is used by many agencies, from different countries. The accomplishments that are made from this support base are world-changing, but never make the news. It might not look like much, but it's importance to a number of operations can't be overstated. Despite that, our visitors to it are not always well-mannered. From coffee spilled on keyboards to secure phones left uncharged to candy bar wrappers littering the table, little annoyances sometimes impede our operational capabilities. So… the existing building will be for the foreigners to make a mess of and then they can deal with their own situations. The new building is ours, exclusively. There will be no outsiders allowed in there, and we will not suffer surprise outages at the hands of those passing through. This station is just too important."*

Esther opened the door- it was thick metal with three locks. There were small windows on the front of the building looking out to the sea, but they were stout glass and too small in size to ever be exploited by someone looking to break in. The inside was cozy, but well laid-out. I would help Esther as best I could to get the network here going, which was only for two desktops, the cameras, a consumer-grade weather station, a cellular repeater, and a Wi-Fi cell for Haitian-use only. John was busy in the other building, and later in the day I would be leaving from this place. It was an interesting few hours, and we accomplished a lot.

This building had its own wireless bridge link back to wherever it originated in Les Cayes, and somehow, they were able to get the most robust Internet uplink I'd seen in Haiti. Esther was a pro by then at setting up the McDermott routers, and she even configured a spare for this location. The PCs were brought online, a couple of different radios were fired up but they went to antennas that would not work very well by my estimation- I helped Esther find the right ones online and we talked about lightning protection that should be added. It was kind of funny, the whole time Esther kept going on about the slobbish activities that happened in the other building, and all the nasty notes she had left trying to get bad habits corrected. The new building would be a temple of order and cleanliness not to be breached by "those traveling man-children".

The day went pretty quickly, and at one point John came in and spoke. *"Howard, please join me in the other building. Your ambassador is on a video call and we need to speak."*

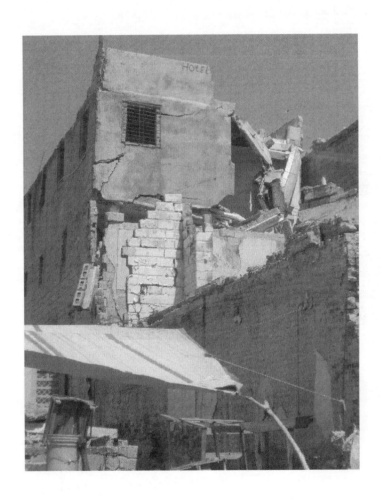

Chapter 14: Getting Back on the Boat

I wasn't quite ready for that invitation, despite telling myself there wasn't much in Haiti that could surprise me anymore. I walked over to the old building, and sure enough I found myself face-to-face with Robert Tillmore, the US Ambassador to Haiti. I fumbled for what to say, and how to great him.

John put me out of my misery. *"Mr. Ambassador, please meet Howard Burlingame. And Mister Howard, I give you your Mr. Ambassador."*

We exchanged pleasantries, and then the Ambassador got right down to business. *"Howard, in just a little while a small low-profile Navy craft will be picking you up. You'll make your way to a larger boat, and then will take a medivac helicopter flight to our naval hospital at Guantanamo. We'll get your head injury looked at there, although the anecdotal evidence is that you're doing OK? John and his team have taken care of you?"*

I agreed that it seemed like I was healing. I was thankful for the care I had received.

"Please listen to me now, and stay with this narrative as you move forward. You were attacked, you have no memory other than the Haitian police finding you alone in a hotel room in Les Cayes. The Embassy had your personal belongings as they were given to us by the hotel, and we got them back to you when you were

on your way to Guantanamo. We happened to have a Navy boat in Les Cayes for minor maintenance, and so it was convenient to get you out of the country that way. Even if you have no lasting damage to your brain, your amnesia on the whole incident will last at least a year, if you don't mind. When your memory comes back, it will be cloudy- you were held at gunpoint and eventually somehow you ended up in a hotel. That's all you know and all you will ever remember- we need to ask that of you. The SIMs for your phones will be returned once you leave Guantanamo in a day or two."

I replied that I understood, and I thanked him. Although I really don't know if he had any part in getting me out of the country or if that was all John's group. I suppose it didn't matter; the Ambassador was certainly at least in the loop.

John added *"Mr. Ambassador understands our arrangement as I described last night, and should you choose to one day tell the story, it will be under an assumed name."*

This was interesting. I didn't feel like I had a lot of say in anything being discussed, so I reverted to being a good soldier. Yes, sir. Will do. Happy to go along, *blah, blah.* I wasn't particularly keen on going to a hospital, and certainly not one at Guantanamo as I just pictured a foreboding prison setting, but whatever. I was on my way home. I thanked Tillmore again, and then John and I had an awkward moment of silence after the screen went dark. He asked me what I was thinking.

"John, have you ever seen the movie *Apocalypse Now?*"

He had, multiple times. It was one of his favorites and he had it on DVD. I told him about my Captain Willard experience when I was attacked, and how I was kind of pissed that I had to get off the boat. John laughed and said that he was glad that I was finally getting back into the boat. I guess I was starting to feel glad, too.

Some people who go to Haiti don't get back to the boat again, ever.

We went back to see how Esther was making out. She had the equipment looking fantastic, and there wasn't much else for us all to do. We drank some bottled water and stayed in the shade of the building watching the birds flying around the shore. John told me that I would get a letter in the future with no return address, and it would tell me how to stay in touch with him. Also, Esther asked if she could occasionally run technical questions and ideas by me, which I was fine with. She told me to watch out for an email from a Canadian university address, with the "subject" of *skateboards*. OK then, count me in on the cloak and dagger stuff.

As we talked, a boat engine could be heard out on the water, and soon we saw a craft approaching. It wasn't what I was expecting, in the least. In my mind, a Navy-gray small military boat would proudly make its way to the dock with flags flying, and a spiffy-looking captain would greet us in his whites. Instead, a very civilian-looking Grady-White cabin cruiser came in like a bat out of hell, and two men in Hawaiian shirts and shorts tied it up. John walked out to them, and I heard him say *"Hello, Mike! How are you? Hello, Mister Randy!"* These men obviously knew John, and they all came walking down the dock with smiles. One of the men took the lead on introductions.

"You must be the Peter Jensen we're here to pick up. I'm Lieutenant Commander Mike O'Brien, This is Senior Petty Officer Randy Grimm." I got the clear impression that Peter Jensen was a code phrase by then. John said *"This Peter Jensen is one of the good guys. Let me introduce Howard Burlingame, friend of Haiti."* I could live with that title. If I was to put a qualifier on it, I would say "friend of the parts of Haiti that don't totally suck", but I kept that thought to myself. I could see that under the flowery shirts, these fellows were armed, and both had handcuffs and various other implements on their belts. I'm assuming they occasionally picked up an unsavory Peter Jensen to whisk off to who knows where. But to see the boat and the men at first glance, they were anything but military. They insisted I call them by their first names.

They both headed to the older building for whatever visitors did in there, and they saw Esther on the way. They all seemed to know each other, and I heard Randy tease her that sooner or later he would get into that new building and spill some coffee and maybe not flush the toilet. She just smiled and held her hand up at him before she came over to talk with me.

Esther said her quick goodbyes. *"I hope we can talk via email, and maybe even on the radio sometime. I hope you remember us with a warm heart."* I told her I would never forget her, or any of this. I mentioned that I'd be happy to show any of them my part of the world if they ever happened to be in New York. She said you never know what might happen. There was a hug, then she touched my head like Nina had. *"You get that checked, rap singer Peter Jensen. You have a good mind and it needs to be healthy. I'm very sorry about your tooth, too."*

I grabbed my bag and Randy took it to the boat. John and Mike came over to me, and John said *"You will like cruising with Mike, Mister Howard. He is the best in the Caribbean. I have learned much from him over the years of our friendship. He gets a little heavy on the throttle though and sometimes the boat is in the air more than it's in the water."* They both smiled.

"Farewell, Mr. Howard. You have your story as described by the Ambassador, and I look forward to the narrative I hope you one day tell about your time

here." We shook hands, and afterwards he gave me a small box to take with me. John saluted Mike- a real salute by one who knows how to do it via military protocol, and Mike returned it as he would for any military staff member. That stuck with me, though I will never really know it's significance. Then off to the boat we went.

Randy said we were about an hour out from the rendezvous point with the next boat and told me to make myself at home. He showed me where the galley was for cold drinks, and where the head was for bathroom business. He said I could wander at will through the boat's thirty-five feet if I was curious about its layout, but to please not touch anything. It was certainly an interesting craft. There was an obvious holding area for the unlucky Peter Jensens of the world, and I'm assuming some decent weapons tucked away somewhere. It was far from new, but it was spotless and very well kept up like any Navy boat would be in the hands of a good crew. After I toured the boat, I opened the box that John had given me. Inside was John's metal Bic lighter he had used to light the cigarettes we had shared. There was also the black bag I'd worn over my head too many times as a "guest". I walked to the back of the boat and threw that in the ocean. Randy watched but said nothing.

The comms gear and radar systems on the boat were fantastic, and most of our run was spent with Randy telling me about it and patiently answering my questions. He was pleased to hear about my Air Force time, as his father was also an airman back in the day. The seas were calm, and the day was sunny- there were perfect conditions for Mike to open the big motors up to show off a bit. That undercover Navy boat could move like a rocket. It was utterly thrilling, and these men were as exotic in the execution of their professions as John was, in their own ways.

We got to the next boat skipping across the ocean without fanfare, and I was surprised that it was a Coast Guard cutter waiting for us rather than a Navy ship. There was a single helicopter on the helipad, and I knew that I would soon be on it heading off for Guantanamo. Mike and Randy got me handed off with kind words and handshakes, and the last I saw of that Grady-White was its impressive wake as Mike took off like a bullet. I kind of envied him in his job at that moment. I was on the cutter just long enough for a medical officer to make sure that I was OK not to be put on a stretcher, then we went to the deck to get on the helicopter. I did a double take when I saw the pilot.

"Dominique- what are you doing here?"

The man looked at me with a flash of recognition, and then said sincerely *"Excuse me, sir? I believe you have me confused with someone else."* I saw his nametag- it said Lt. Commander Vincent. We locked eyes, and I could almost feel him willing me to simply shut up. Then the medical officer introduced me to Marvin- the pilot. *"You just came from Haiti, right Mr. Burlingame? Marvin has a twin brother there who also flies helicopters for some private company. It's a small world at times…"*

Wow. Many lights went on for just then. Marvin and Dominique were twins, and with the last name of Vincent, they were likely brothers or cousins to Ekselan Junior Vincent. That was pretty wild, and my Haiti world got smaller just then. I boarded and took my assigned seat in the back next to a medic crewmember. The medical thing was getting overly played up, I thought. Or perhaps the military folks had just been given information that a wounded American needed transport. My vitals were taken a couple of times in the flight, and it just felt odd, but then again this whole trip was one for the books. I didn't have that much of a window view from where I sat, and there wasn't a lot of chatter among the crew. I did not have a headset like when I flew with Dominique, and I saw my escort say almost nothing into his microphone. The trip was fairly uneventful for probably forty-five minutes. I started to get glimpses of land off in the far distance, and then the Coast Guardsman by my side held his headset out to me. He shouted over the engine noise *"Commander Vincent would like a private word with you, sir."*

I put the headset on, and I saw the other two crew members take theirs off. Then Marvin spoke. *"Mister Howard, I have heard some of the details of your adventures of the last week or so. You have seen much that outsiders are not meant to see."* He paused, and I didn't know what to say. I was kind of dull-minded right then, and I hadn't been expecting this conversation. I simply said "copy that", and Marvin continued. *"Thank you for your assistance to my family, and to the organization. And thank you for your open mindedness."* Again, I struggled for words. All I came up with was "you're welcome, Sir. They are good people." He closed the dialogue with *"you are obviously a man of action and character. The world needs more of them. Travel safe to your home, Sir. Please put my corpsman back on."* I had questions about who all was in Marvin's family out of the men and women I'd spent time with, but those would have to remain unanswered. And here I thought the most incredible story ended when I left Les Cayes.

As we came upon Guantanamo, Cuba was incredible looking from above. Lush in the sun, it looked simply beautiful to me. Guantanamo Bay was not what I expected, although I can't say that I really knew what I expected. The bay as a geographical feature is sort of a collection of jagged fingers and channels of water, and the whole thing winds inland at strange angles rather than just being a simple opening of the land to the sea. It was striking to see from the air, and our decent in did give me some nice glimpses when the helicopter banked just right. As I thought about all I'd seen and heard in Haiti, I understood why an American military presence was strategic on Cuba for reaching the Caribbean and even South America .

Marvin put us down gently on the hospital's helipad so softly I didn't realize we were on the ground, and he kept the motor running while I got out. I got a quick wave from him and the rest of the crew as I was put in a wheelchair, and then my last connection to a fascinating group of people headed back into the sky.

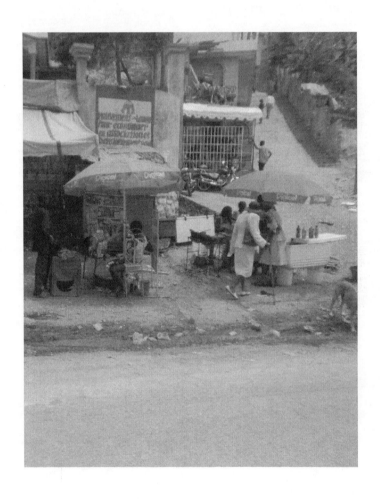

Chapter 15: The Aftermath

The medical folks at Guantanamo were beyond kind and considerate. They treated me like a dignitary for the roughly seventy-two hours I was there. The scans showed that I did in fact have a traumatic brain injury, and that it was healing as well as they would hope. It was surreal looking at the image of my own brain. There was a mild skull fracture and a hell of a bruise that even I could discern never having looked at a brain that way.

I stuck with the amnesia story as agreed to, and the doctor said that "it all might come back" at some point, or perhaps I'd never remember the specifics of the attack and the events that followed it. Given that I actually remembered every minute of Haiti, it was a little uncomfortable living a lie. But I had agreed to that and so I did my best acting. They also had an oral surgeon take a look at my broken molar, and he declared it would need an implant given the extensive damage from the attack. (Eventually workers comp insurance covered that whole thing, and the McDermott folks were great in seeing that I got everything related to the tooth dealt with.) I was feeling all right with everything the Guantanamo folks told me, and I had some surprisingly decent hospital chow. It was nothing on the order of what Nina fed me, but it was good to have American food again.

My second night there, an odd thing happened. I had my first of what would become a fairly frequent nightmare, or flashback, or whatever you want to call it.

I had eaten, walked around a bit, showered, and watched TV before going to bed. At some point in the night, I had just an utterly terrible dream. It was essentially a vivid rerun of the attack in Port-au-Prince, with the worst parts amplified to the point where I was gripped by terror. I must have yelled in my sleep, because a slightly freaked out nurse woke me up. She was young enough to be my daughter, but was great at talking with me about what I had just had playing out in my mind. She spent maybe a half-hour with me, just listening to my story in the wee hours, and then I went back to sleep without further event. The next day the doctor said it was akin to PTSD or flashbacks, and there might be more to come with some undetermined frequency.

After another day of observation, I caught a ride on an Air Force transport to the big base in New Jersey. Somewhere over the Carolinas, a female captain walked back to where I was sitting from the cockpit, made a little small talk, and then handed me the sim cards for my phones in a ziplock bag. I realized the phones were both pretty much dead, as I hadn't even thought about using them until then. The captain went and retrieved her own battery bank for me to use for the rest of the flight, which was really kind of her. After we landed, I got a taxi to the Newark airport for my flight back to Rochester. I had a couple of hours to kill, so I called my parents and a few different people to update them on my status. They had been told by the State Department when to expect me back, and I'd end up with a small welcoming party at Rochester when I eventually got back. I opted to email Claude at McDermott rather than calling him, as I just wasn't up to talking with him or anyone else from the university yet.

And then I was home, and eventually back to work. It took me around a week to want to engage again. I felt like I had been gone a year and had the shit kicked out of me both mentally and physically.

Weeks went by, as did months. Several surgeries later, I had a spiffy new titanium dental implant. I was having the flashback nightmare thing maybe once or twice a month, usually it was just unpleasant enough to wake me up. Other times it was absolutely fucking terrifying and I had to fight to get my body to let me wake to escape it. That seems to be something that will be with me maybe for life, as it hasn't abated much, years after the fact. I'm living with it though and now have a very real appreciation for those other folks out there dealing with PTSD.

I had a number of follow ups with a neurologist and a couple of other doctors in those first several months home. The brain thing healed for the most part, but I still get sudden migraines that radiate from the site of the injury if I get stressed, so I try not to get stressed.

Several people encouraged me to sue McDermott over the whole mess, but that isn't my style. I know that I did not have to go to Haiti; I went willingly even if I tried to raise flags about the wisdom along the way. McDermott has been good to me, and if nothing else, Haiti gave me war stories to tell. Like this book- which was written to fulfill John's request.

I did leave the University after a couple of years, as I was having trouble managing the headaches when deep into complicated networking projects. I retired with what can only be called a disability, and now I generally do hobby activities, small IT jobs for friends, and volunteer work. It is what it is.

I did eventually hear from John, and I do stay in touch with him. We have become long-distance friends, and I value the relationship. Since my stay with him, there have been a handful of presidents come and gone for Haiti, and John has always had a unique perspective on each one to share. That time in his house, with his team, was so intense for me that I don't imagine I'll lose interest in revisiting it in my mind until I'm an old man. Esther also has reached out, and we communicate far less frequently than with John, and it's usually about her technical challenges but occasionally we get chummy about some silly thing. She is doing incredible work with various technologies, and I'm not at liberty to get into those specifics.

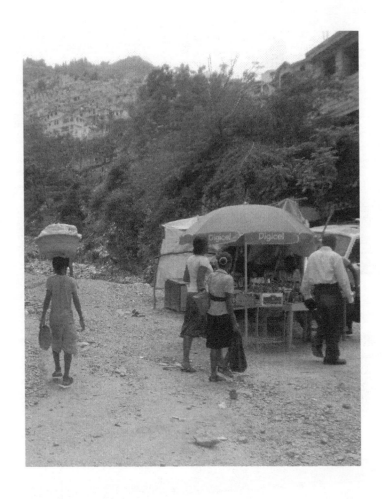

Conclusion- What's in a Name?

As I mentioned, I very much stay in contact with John. He often relays the high-level details of what is going on with various "guests" in his house without giving too much away. Usually, he and Nina are hosts to some pretty rotten eggs. There was a Dominican human trafficker, preying on young Haitian schoolgirls. And the fake UN soldier from Brazil who turned out to actually be a Haitian gang leader trying to corrupt real UN soldiers into all kinds of shady activities. Or the politician gangster whose dealings got too many innocent Haitians killed along the way as he conducted all sorts of mob-level stuff out of his political office. John sees all kinds of bad guys, and he stays an absolute gentleman somehow through it all. Rarely bitter, he always feels upbeat to me despite the load he carries.

He did relay that an unsavory character tried to attack Nina one day in the very room I slept in, and they picked up his body from the ground below the balcony. Nina and I drank beer on that balcony, and her and Esther danced to Ekselan Junior while John and I bullshitted and smoked cigarettes there. But this man decided to try to take on Nina, and she sent him to the ground from the balcony with a couple of bloody gashes from her razor as parting gifts. I think it helps John somewhat to share it all with someone who was there, as I was.

One thing I tease John about is what his group might be named. He assures me that they do have a name and have since the organization's inception several generations ago. It just isn't known to anyone outside of the group- not even to confidants like myself. I ask him things like "how's it going for the Guardians of Liberty?" or "Have the Haitian Knights of Hip Hop prevented any assassinations lately?" He just goes with it, always with a witty comeback. He says he writes them all down, and if their leadership ever decides they need a new name, he'll be ready with all the wonderful ideas that I've given him. His personal favorite so far is The East Side of the Island Cowboys (and Cowgirls) for Justice.

He's got a great sense of humor.

Why This Story?

I travelled to Haiti twice as part of the many who wanted to help the country to recover after the devastating earthquake. On the second trip. I did end up in a protest zone, and I was injured. More than a decade later, I still do have the occasional nightmare about it, as I have nightmares on occasion about experiences from my time in the military. This book- this *story-* is a gift to myself. I took the situation of my time in Haiti back, and reshaped it in a fictional way that pleases me while preserving many of the essences of the trip as I experienced them.

Thank you for reading.

Other works from Lee Badman

The Whales of Yellowstone: One Man's Life as a Discotheque Clubbing Icon and Fashion God

Echoes From My Military Past

Cross Lake Tales for Grown-Ups

Even More Cross Lake tales for Grown-Ups

Made in the USA
Columbia, SC
08 June 2023